Darling Remy,

This will be my last letter to you and I know you will understand why. Remy, I have grown to love William and I know you will wish me well. Here is a man who loves me and whom I can love without diminishing what I felt—what a part of me will always feel—for you. How lucky can one woman be?

But it's too soon for me to sit back and enjoy this newfound happiness. Charlotte and I are being pressured to sell the hotel by men who would rather see it ruined than remain in our hands.

It's crazy, Remy, but no matter how bad things become, there is always a ray of hope. Are you using your influence to make things brighter for us, mon cher? That's the first thing I thought of when Charlotte's old beau, Jackson Bailey, showed up in the midst of our troubles. If we owe this to your intervention, then don't stop now—at least not until our Charlotte has found her own love.

No matter what happens, my promise to you holds true. I will do everything in my power to ensure that our life's dream, the Hotel Marchand, will survive.

Forever your love,

Anne

Dear Reader,

Unmasked is a story about believing in magic. Now, I don't mean the abracadabra, pull-a-rabbit-from-a-hat kind of magic, I'm talking about that illogical, little leap of faith that powers every dream.

Of course, convincing a hyper-responsible, velvet steamroller of a character like Charlotte Marchand to believe in anything other than the bottom line wasn't easy. It was almost as challenging as persuading the globe-trotting Dr. Jackson Bailey that he could indeed go home again. Still, what better place for Charlotte and Jackson to rediscover the magic of love than in New Orleans at Mardi Gras?

For me that required another leap of faith. Along with most of the world, I watched in horror as Hurricane Katrina turned the American Gulf Coast into a disaster zone. In particular, the devastation suffered by New Orleans was difficult to fathom. As I wrote *Unmasked,* the rebuilding efforts were still in their early stages. I hope with all my heart that by the time you read these words, the magic that defined the Big Easy will have returned.

Sincerely,

Ingrid

INGRID WEAVER
Unmasked

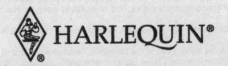

TORONTO • NEW YORK • LONDON
AMSTERDAM • PARIS • SYDNEY • HAMBURG
STOCKHOLM • ATHENS • TOKYO • MILAN • MADRID
PRAGUE • WARSAW • BUDAPEST • AUCKLAND

ISBN-13: 978-0-373-38945-2
ISBN-10:   0-373-38945-0

UNMASKED

Copyright © 2006 by Harlequin Books S.A.

Ingrid Weaver is acknowledged as the author of this work.

Ingrid Weaver propped an old manual typewriter on her children's playroom table to write her first novel. Twenty-two books later there's a computer in place of the typewriter and a RITA® Award on the corner of her grown-up-sized desk, but the joy she found in creating her first story hasn't changed. "I write because life is full of possibilities," Ingrid says, "and the best ones are those that we make." She is an avid gardener in the summer and a knitter in the winter. Ingrid lives on a farm, just a short drive from Toronto. You can visit Ingrid's Web site at www.ingridweaver.com.

CHAPTER ONE

THE MARDI GRAS MASK was a whimsical concoction of white feathers and sequins. Scarcely longer than Charlotte's hand, it shimmered as it rested on her palm, as weightless—and as fragile—as the trace of a kiss. It was meant to be an adornment, not a disguise, designed to evoke a fairy-tale princess.

Of course, fairy tales were for children, as impractical as make-believe and as implausible as happy endings. A person had to find their own luck, just as they had to guide their own fate. Charlotte Marchand had learned long ago that the real world made no allowance for weaknesses, and she couldn't permit herself any now.

But dear God, she wished she could still believe in magic.

Charlotte blinked, surprised to feel the sting of tears. She pressed her lips together and breathed deeply through her nose until the urge to weep passed. She wouldn't permit herself to fall apart, even here in the privacy of her office. That was a luxury she couldn't afford.

Resolutely she placed the mask on the corner of her desk and focused on the stack of printouts in front of her. It was late, and she'd been at the hotel since daybreak, but she still had work to do before she could go home. Somewhere in that pile of numbers there had to be a solution, and it was up to her to find it.

The week before Mardi Gras was traditionally the busiest tourist season of the year, the make-or-break time for the New Orleans hospitality business. This year more than ever, countless jobs depended on making it a success. But at the Hotel Marchand, bookings were on a downward spiral. The string of problems that had plagued them over the past several weeks had driven away customers and wiped out their profits. The Marchand family finances had been stretched to the breaking point and couldn't prop up the business indefinitely. Charlotte needed to turn things around within the next seven days or the hotel likely wouldn't see another Mardi Gras.

Then again, people flocked to Mardi Gras in order to forget their troubles and cut loose. It was a celebration of possibilities, when anything could happen.

Just this once, why shouldn't it happen for her?

The mask caught the glow of the desk lamp, setting off a flash of sequins. The feathers shifted on some current of air that Charlotte couldn't feel, making it look as if they stirred on their own, as if by magic...

She hesitated, then extended her hand to run a fingertip along the edge of a feather.

Forgetting troubles never solved them. She'd learned that around the same time she'd given up hoping her own fairy tale would come true.

Pressure built in her throat, but she wasn't sure whether it was from more tears or from an irrational urge to laugh.

Magic? Fairy tales? What was wrong with her tonight? Maybe the strain of trying to keep the hotel afloat was finally catching up to her. She never indulged in whimsy. She was sensible, responsible Charlotte, always doing the right thing and obeying every rule. She strove to be a good daughter and grand-daughter, sister and aunt, putting others first, whatever the cost.

Fine, that was all well and good, but when was it going to be *her* turn?

"Just this once," she whispered. "Would a little magic be too much to ask?"

As if in reply, the hush of her office was shattered by the shriek of the fire alarm.

Charlotte's hand jerked, knocking the mask to the floor. No. Please. Let this be a glitch in the wiring system or a prank by a tipsy guest. She grabbed her cell phone and dialed the number for security. "Mac!" She jammed the phone to her ear, trying to hear over the noise of the alarm. "What's going on?"

Mac Jensen was in his last week as head of the hotel's security. He'd agreed to stay on until the end of Mardi Gras, but Charlotte knew he was eager to return to his own security business. "A smoke detector in the maintenance area was triggered," he replied. His voice was uneven—he sounded as if he were running. "I'm heading there now."

She slid her feet back into her shoes and went to the window behind her desk. Except for the echoing alarm, the courtyard below seemed just as it would on any normal evening. Tiny lights winked from the trees, softening the shadows beneath. Amid the scattered lounge chairs and tables, the pool glowed serenely, an elegant oasis in the center of the hotel. She slipped her phone into the pocket of her suit jacket, braced her hands on the windowsill and leaned outward to get a better view.

The doors to the hotel bar burst open. People streamed into the courtyard, some knocking over chairs in their haste as they headed for the alley to the street. A white-haired man fell, creating a jostling pileup behind him. Within seconds one of the cocktail waitresses had helped him up, while more staff members directed the crowd toward the exits.

The employees of the Hotel Marchand were well drilled in emergency procedures, so their first priority was the safety of the guests and of themselves. Mac had said a detector had been triggered in the maintenance area, which was in the same wing as the bar and the hotel's kitchen. There was a chance that some leftover cooking fumes had set it off by mistake.

Black smoke puffed through the open bar doors. That explained the mass scramble to evacuate. This was no false alarm.

Charlotte spun from the window and headed for the corridor. At least her family was safe. Her sisters weren't working tonight; lately they had been spending every spare minute with their new fiancés. Her mother wasn't here either—Anne would be at the hospital with William, *her* new fiancé. They were all trusting Charlotte to take care of the hotel....

She moaned under her breath. This couldn't be as bad as it looked, could it?

The lobby was clogged with people, most pushing their way toward the street, but some who were dressed in their nightclothes were milling around and obviously confused. Julie Sullivan, Charlotte's administrative assistant, stood in the center of the melee, doing her best to spread calm in spite of the bone-jarring shriek of the alarm.

"Miss Marchand," someone called. "I demand an explanation."

Charlotte assumed an expression of confidence that she didn't come close to feeling and turned toward the voice. She recognized a pair of the Hotel Marchand's longtime patrons—

the couple had reserved the same suite during Mardi Gras since they had honeymooned here and hadn't missed a year yet. "I'm sorry for the inconvenience, Mr. Shore. We'll have everyone back in their rooms as soon as possible. But in the meantime, you'll both need to move outside."

He put his arm around the tiny woman beside him and guided her toward the front door. "This never would have happened in the old days when your parents were in charge," he said over his shoulder.

Somehow Charlotte maintained her smile as she sweetened her apology with the promise of a complimentary meal.

She continued through the crowd, soothing the guests and encouraging the staff. She knew there was no need to panic. Like the other buildings in the historic French Quarter, the Hotel Marchand was old, yet it had withstood the worst that man and nature could throw at it for almost two centuries. The hotel's alarm was hardwired to the New Orleans 911 system, so fire trucks would already be en route. Between the continuing alarm bleats, she was sure she heard distant sirens. Several of the hotel's uniformed security staff were at the front entrance to keep order outside and to direct the firemen when they arrived. Everything was going according to the emergency plan.

Yet the panic was there, just beneath the surface, and no amount of logic could combat it.

The hotel was more than bricks and mortar to Charlotte, far more than just a means to make a living. It was the focus of her life. Her anchor and her refuge.

She'd known she was in danger of losing it but not so soon. *Mon Dieu*, not like this.

AT THE FIRST WHIFF OF smoke, even before the alarm sounded, Jackson could feel his nape prickle and his pulse slam against the scar tissue in his hand. Yet he never considered going the other way. As the rest of the bar patrons scrambled for the exits, he headed straight in the direction where the smoke was the thickest.

He wasn't alone. Two security men, both carrying fire extinguishers, pushed through to the service hallway ahead of him. Shouts came from the far end, where more figures moved in the haze. The overhead sprinklers came on with a whoosh, cutting through the smoke that had gathered near the ceiling, but fresh clouds rolled from an open doorway midway down the corridor.

Someone caught his elbow from behind. "Sir! You can't come back here."

Jackson looked over his shoulder. The man who had stopped him didn't wear a uniform, but it was obvious by his bearing that he belonged to the hotel security staff. Instead of a fire extinguisher, he held a cell phone. Like everyone else Jackson had encountered so far tonight, he was a stranger.

Yet it had been almost twenty years since he had set foot in the Hotel Marchand. The building had remained the same, but he'd known that the people in it were bound to change. "You might need my help," he said.

The man swept Jackson with an impatient glance, taking in his shaggy hair, faded denim and well-worn boots. "Thanks, but—"

"I'm a doctor."

There was the sharp pop of a small explosion, followed by shouts and a fresh billow of orange-tinged smoke.

Swearing, the security man released Jackson's elbow and sprinted down the hall.

The fire was in a storage room lined with shelves of stacked linens, cardboard boxes and bottles of what likely were cleaning fluids. From the doorway Jackson could see pieces of broken plastic near the bottles—one of them must have burst from the heat, causing the explosion he'd heard.

Water from the sprinklers hissed and turned to steam as it fell, tamping down the smoke that curled from the shelves. But it wasn't enough to douse the flames that roared from a blackened heap of towels in the center of the floor. The men with the fire extinguishers advanced on the blaze, trying to contain it beneath a layer of white foam. Jackson stayed a safe distance back and surveyed the rest of the scene, automatically searching for any injured.

A young man with sandy blond hair leaned against one of the shelves beside the doorway. Moisture glistened from the soot that streaked his face and plastered his white shirt to his shoulders. He stared at the flames, his gaze bleak, a charred gray suit coat—the same kind the hotel staff wore—gripped in his hands. He seemed unaware of the blood that dripped from his cuff.

Jackson yanked a handful of linen napkins from a stack near the door and touched the man's arm to get his attention. He shouted over the noise. "Let's go outside. I need to take a look at that cut."

The man didn't move. "I tried to put it out." His voice was rough. "I swear, I tried."

Rather than dragging him out by force, Jackson lifted the man's wrist and peeled back his sleeve. A gash on his forearm welled crimson. It appeared to be a clean cut, probably from a piece of flying plastic. He pressed a napkin to the wound. "Hold this."

"I got here too late. I never thought it would be this bad." He glanced at his arm, then dropped his charred coat and slapped his hand over the makeshift compress.

Jackson wrapped it in a second napkin. Silently cursing his clumsy fingers, he leaned over and used his teeth to tighten the ends into a knot. "You'll need to get that disinfected and stitched."

One of the uniformed security men cried out and dropped his fire extinguisher. He leaped backward, beating at the flames that raced up his pant leg, but he couldn't stop the fabric from igniting. Instantly his legs were engulfed in a cone of orange.

Jackson grabbed some sheets from a shelf and flung them around the man's legs to smother the flames, then enlisted the help of the blond man to haul the injured security guard outside. Between them they got him to the fresh air of the courtyard and laid him on one of the lounge chairs beside the pool where the light was the strongest.

Given the circumstances, Jackson was capable of administering only the most basic first aid, but he reasoned that was better than nothing. He improvised, using what was available to minimize the trauma to the guard's burned skin and to keep him from going into shock. Within minutes, the fire department arrived amid a chorus of sirens. Soon afterward an ambulance drove through the lane to the courtyard. As the paramedics hooked up an IV drip, Jackson got on their radio to ensure a burn specialist would be waiting at the hospital.

He fell into the rhythm of the crisis easily, never noticing when the alarm shut off. Gradually the pace of activity slowed. As the smoke that hung in the air began to clear, word spread that the fire was out. It had been minor to begin with, and the quick actions of the hotel staff had prevented it from spreading. Some of the men who had initially battled the blaze were given a few minutes of oxygen, but none had been exposed to the smoke long enough to require further treatment. Mercifully there were no other injuries.

"We'll take it from here, Doctor. Thanks for the help."

Jackson nodded and moved aside as the burn victim was loaded into the ambulance. The paramedics had the situation under control and were already packing up their gear, so there was nothing more he could do without getting in the way. He flexed his fingers, frustrated by his limitations but grateful that he'd been able to do as much as he had.

He waited until the ambulance was safely on its way, then walked to the table in the shadows where he'd discarded his denim jacket.

"Excuse me, sir?" The security man who had tried to stop Jackson earlier was hurrying around the pool toward him. Like the others who had been first on the scene, his face was tinged with soot.

"Yes?"

"I'm Mac Jensen, head of hotel security." He held out his hand. "Thanks for your help back there."

Not wanting to risk the damage from a hard squeeze, Jackson kept his jacket in his right hand and grasped Mac's hand briefly with his left. "Jackson Bailey. And you're welcome. Barring complications, everyone should make a full recovery."

"That's what I heard. We were lucky."

"You appeared well prepared."

"Yeah, those fire drills paid off." He did a quick survey of the area. "Where's Carter?"

"Who?"

"Luc Carter, our concierge. You bandaged his arm."

Jackson glanced around but couldn't see the blond man anywhere. "Carter helped me with the man who was burned. He must have gone with the ambulance."

"I'll catch up with him later. Are you a guest here, Dr. Bailey?"

"Yes, I checked in tonight."

"This wasn't much of a welcome." His gaze went past Jackson's shoulder. "We'll see what the hotel can do to show our appreciation," he added, lifting his arm as if to get some-one's attention.

Jackson shrugged on his jacket. "That's not necessary. I only did what anyone…" His words trailed off. Over the drone of activity from the remaining firemen and the chatter of the guests who were trickling back inside, Jackson thought he could hear the tap of high heels on the courtyard's paving stones.

And for the second time that night his pulse tripped and the hair at his nape tingled. But it wasn't from dread, it was from anticipation.

How was it possible that after all these years he still recog-nized the sound of her walk? Her steps were the light, rapid stride of a petite woman. Although she moved quickly, he knew she wouldn't appear to hurry. Charlotte Marchand had too much grace for that.

"What's your take on the damage, Mac?"

The words were laced with anxiety, businesslike and to

the point. Yet Charlotte's voice was as distinctive as her walk—and it hadn't changed either. Echoes stirred in his mind: her laughter as they snatched a beignet from the hotel's kitchen, her voice on the phone late at night, husky with sleep. She'd always been too stubborn to be the first one to say goodbye.

He turned to face her…and felt as if he'd been punched.

The walk and the voice might be the same, but this wasn't the girl he remembered. Where were her curls? The round cheeks and earnest grin? Her poise was as unruffled as her silk suit and her makeup. She could have been serving tea in her grandmother's parlor instead of standing amid the aftermath of a fire.

"It was confined to the housekeeping storeroom," Mac said. "Some supplies were lost, but it wasn't as bad as it looked at first. The cleanup won't take long."

"Thank God. Where's Emilio? I was told he was burned."

Jackson spoke before Mac could reply. "He's on his way to Mercy Hospital. The burns were serious but not life-threatening. He should make a full recovery."

She looked at him, her expression settling into the polite smile one would give a stranger.

Jackson stared, still trying to absorb what he was seeing. While Charlotte had been pretty, this woman had a sleek, bone-deep beauty that stole his breath. Her green gaze was as steady as it always had been, yet her almond-shaped eyes seemed more exotic than before. The delicate features that had once haunted his teenage fantasies had firmed with the ripe confidence of maturity.

This wasn't the same girl who had broken his heart.

On the other hand, he sure as hell wasn't the same boy. He

tilted his head, one corner of his mouth lifting in a smile. "Hello, Charlie."

The nickname made her start. Recognition flashed through her eyes. *"Jackson?"*

"Dr. Bailey got to the fire the same time I did," Mac said. "He jumped right in and started giving first aid. I was going to introduce you, but I see you already know each other."

She answered without taking her gaze from Jackson. "That's right, Mac. Dr. Bailey and I are old friends."

Friends? It was a civilized description, though not entirely accurate. It went along with this new polished and poised version of Charlotte. "I heard you're running the hotel now," Jackson said. "Congratulations."

"Thank you. I realize it doesn't look its best at the moment but—"

"The place looks great. Just as I remember."

"It's been through a lot the past year and a half."

"So have you." He lifted his good hand to brush a lock of hair from her cheek. "How are you doing?"

The gesture had been automatic, unthinking, another one of those echoes from the past, but it had the same effect as his use of her old nickname. She jerked back before he could touch her, then covered her movement with a light cough. "We're all fine, thanks. How are your parents? I understand they're in Iowa now."

He dropped his hand to his side. "They're doing fine."

"I'm glad to hear it. And thank you for stepping in to help us tonight."

"I did what I could."

"This must have been tame compared to what you're ac-

customed to doing. Are you still working with aid organiza-
tions overseas?"

They hadn't seen each other in twenty years, Jackson
thought, and they were talking about their jobs.

Well, what had he expected? A tearful reunion? That
wasn't why he'd come home. "Yes, I am, whenever I can
fit the trips into my hospital schedule. My last stint was in
Afghanistan."

"What brings you back to New Orleans now…?" She drew
in her breath. "Oh, I should have realized. You must be here
to see your uncle William."

Before he could decide how to reply, a phone started to
ring. There was no opportunity for any further conversation.
Charlotte murmured an apology to him and took a small silver
cell phone from her pocket. By the time she finished the call,
a uniformed policewoman had approached and begun to ask
questions. They were joined by the fire chief and a large man
in a business suit who said he was a detective.

Charlotte handled them all with smooth professional-
ism and her tea-in-the-parlor graciousness. Jackson was im-
pressed, but he knew he shouldn't be surprised. Running the
Hotel Marchand was what she'd been born and raised for. It
was what she'd always wanted.

Yet there'd once been a time when she'd wanted more.

Another memory raced through his mind, a vivid rush of
innocence and first love. Instead of the competent stranger in
ivory silk and pearls, he saw the girl who used to lean her head
on his shoulder and whisper her dreams.

And regardless of the crowd that separated them, in spite
of all the years that had passed, he wanted to reach out and

pull her into his arms. She used to fit into his embrace so naturally they'd both believed she would be there forever....

Frowning, Jackson slipped his hands into his pockets. What was wrong with him tonight? The strain of the past few weeks must be catching up. Starting anything with Charlotte now was the last thing he needed. Besides, forever was for fairy tales, just like happy endings, and he'd stopped believing in those a long time ago.

THE SOLITARY FIGURE threaded his way between the cartons that were stacked on the warehouse floor, his blond hair gleaming as he passed through a pool of light. Above him, behind the bulletproof glass that enclosed the Cajun Syrup Company's office, Mike Blount observed the man's approach in silence until his footsteps rang on the steel staircase. Mike snapped his fingers and pointed to the office door. "Show him in, Richard."

Richard Corbin took a long drag on what was left of his cigarette. He knocked off the ashes with a nervous flick and glanced toward the corner where his brother stood.

The way Dan Corbin posed with his ankles crossed and one elbow propped on the top of a filing cabinet seemed casual, but the muscle that jumped in his cheek betrayed his tension. He tucked his tie into his jacket and moved his head in an almost imperceptible nod.

Mike narrowed his eyes at the silent byplay. Didn't they yet realize who was in charge? Without the timely infusion of cash Mike had provided, by now the Corbins' crooked hotel business would have collapsed and the law would have caught up to them. They owed him big-time, and he wasn't planning to cut them loose until they delivered what they'd promised. He waited as Richard went to do what he was told, then clasped his hands over his stomach and leaned back in his chair to assess the new arrival.

As the concierge of the Hotel Marchand, Luc Carter should have been in an ideal position to sabotage the hotel undetected. Mike needed to decide whether Carter was as unreliable as the Corbin brothers claimed or merely a convenient scapegoat for their own incompetence.

"Why are we meeting here, Richard?" Carter demanded as he stepped into the office. "Since when were you in the pancake syrup business?"

"This building belongs to me, Mr. Carter," Mike said. "And my interests extend far beyond the syrup business."

Carter spun toward his voice, frowning into the shadows beyond the desk lamp where Mike sat. "Who are you?"

He must have come straight from the fire, Mike thought. The scent of smoke rolled from his clothes and his shirt was soiled with soot and dried blood. The only clean thing on him was the gauze bandage that wrapped his forearm.

Keeping his gaze on Carter, Mike lifted one hand to gesture toward Dan. "I'll let him explain."

Dan pushed away from the filing cabinet and cleared his throat. "This is Mike Blount. He has an interest in the hotel."

"What does that mean?"

"A future interest," Dan said. "Once we acquire the hotel from the Marchand family, we're going to transfer the ownership to Mike."

Carter looked from Dan to Richard. "I don't understand. We had a deal."

Richard took a pack of cigarettes from his pocket, shook out a fresh one and lit it from the end of the butt he held. "Yeah, but we made a deal with Mike," he said. "And since you have a deal with us, that makes you part of it."

"That's not what I agreed. What—"

"You claimed you could run down the business to the point where the Marchands would have to sell it," Dan said. "Who ends up with the hotel isn't the issue. Your lack of success is."

"I told you I'd handle the fire myself," Carter said. "It was supposed to be minor."

"What happened to your arm, Luc?" Mike asked.

Carter shifted to face him. He was a handsome man—no doubt the ladies found his blue eyes and Ken-doll looks charming. "Some cleaning fluid exploded," he said, pulling his wrist against his chest. "And I'm not the only one who was injured. Setting the fire in that storeroom was a mistake."

"It's like I said," Richard muttered. "He's got no guts."

"It has nothing to do with guts," Carter said. "It's about brains. No one was supposed to get hurt. That's going to attract too much attention from the authorities."

"Let me worry about the authorities," Mike said.

"You should have waited for me," Carter persisted. "The point of that fire was to hurt the business, not burn the place to the ground."

"We didn't set it," Richard said. "That was Mike's people."

Carter took a step toward the desk. "You? Why?"

"I'm accustomed to getting results," Mike said. "From what my associates here have told me, so far all you've done is create a few nuisances."

"The strategy was effective. Business is down."

"And yet the Marchand women still refuse to sell. It's time to step things up."

"I've gotten to know the Marchands over the past few months. The more you push, the more stubborn they'll get."

"Here's the thing, Luc." Mike's chair creaked as he leaned forward and brought his face into the light. "What your friends here might not have made clear enough is that we're working on a deadline. I expect to acquire the Hotel Marchand by the end of Mardi Gras."

"That's only a week away." He glanced at the Corbins. "I told them—we need more time."

Mike drummed his fingers against his desk. "The Corbins believe you're stalling."

A sheen of sweat appeared on Carter's forehead. "Why would I do that?"

"Perhaps Richard is right and you have no stomach for a more direct approach."

"I'm telling you it won't work. You need to have patience."

"When it comes to the Hotel Marchand, I've been a very patient man," Mike said. Without taking his gaze from Carter, he pulled open the top drawer of his desk and took out one of his knives. He'd come a long way from skinning muskrats in the Atchafalaya, but he still had a fondness for the tools his papa had taught him to use in the swamp. He stroked the flat of the blade with his thumb. "The Corbins made me a promise, Luc. And it would be in your best interests to make sure they're able to keep it."

CHAPTER TWO

CHARLOTTE PUSHED OPEN the door to the Hotel Marchand's kitchen, pausing to savor the aromas of cooling pastry and roasting coffee beans. Butter sizzled, a timer chimed and pots clanged in a familiar din that took her back to her childhood. While the kitchen had been expanded and upgraded over the years, the smells and sounds that filled it hadn't changed. She'd grown up with them, and they never failed to steady her. "You're a darling, Keisha," she said into her phone. "I appreciate your help."

"The first batch of sheets will be coming out of the tumblers in five minutes, Miss Charlotte. I'll have the van there in an hour."

"I knew I could count on you."

"Hold on. This is going to cost you extra."

Charlotte tried not to wince. Despite the red ink on the printouts in her office, she'd extended her offer of a free meal to all the guests who had been inconvenienced by the previous night's fire. From what she could see, the entire kitchen staff was hard at work already, frantically preparing complimentary breakfasts. But the free food wouldn't keep her customers happy for long if there were no clean sheets or towels. "Whatever you want, Keisha. Name your price."

A low laugh came through the phone. "Now, Miss Charlotte, don't sound so worried. You and Miss Anne helped me keep my business going through hell and high water, and I got no plan to bankrupt you now. All I want is some of that chocolate turkey your sister makes. The kind with the feta cheese and cayenne."

"Done. I'll send someone over with it tonight."

"With extra feta?"

"It will be swimming in it, I promise." She terminated the call, then leaned one shoulder against a storage cabinet and rubbed her eyes. If only she could solve the rest of the details on her to-do list with more food.

The night had been endless. From the time the fire had been extinguished it seemed as if she'd been doing nothing but putting out countless others. She'd managed to squeeze in a hasty trip home an hour ago for a bath and a change of clothes, but the problems had started again the moment she'd returned to the hotel.

A light touch on her arm made her jump. Charlotte opened her eyes and quickly straightened up.

Melanie, her youngest sister, was studying her with concern. "Have you slept at all?" she asked.

"Of course." The lie was automatic—she wasn't accustomed to having the baby of the family worrying about her big sister instead of the other way around. "Thanks so much for coming into work early."

"I don't know how you do it, Charlotte." Melanie shook her head, her ponytail swinging. "You look better after an all-nighter than I do after a full eight hours."

"You're too kind," Charlotte said, and she meant it. With

her dramatic coloring and tall, slender figure, Melanie didn't need makeup or designer clothes to make an impact. She couldn't have looked bad if she'd tried. "But after that lovely compliment, it's going to be difficult to ask you another favor."

"Name it."

"I promised Keisha some of your chocolate turkey in exchange for her putting a rush on the laundry."

"That won't be a problem. Robert and I have things here under control."

There was a sharp clang of something hitting the floor, accompanied by a spurt of French curses as one of Robert LeSoeur's assistants raced to get a mop. Charlotte leaned to the side in order to see what had happened, but Melanie moved to block her view. "Don't worry, we really do have everything under control."

"The cleaning crew hadn't finished in the restaurant when I arrived. The smoke seems to have tainted everything."

"That's already taken care of. We won't be using Chez Remy. We're setting up a buffet outside."

"It might be too cool."

"It's a gorgeous morning. The temperature's already warming up." She took Charlotte's arm and gently steered her out of the kitchen. "Come and see."

Charlotte breathed a sigh of relief as soon as she and Melanie reached the courtyard. Here, in the shelter of the buildings, the air was mild, and there was no hint of smoke to mar it. The furniture that had been toppled or pushed aside had been righted. Birds trilled and darted through the treetops, where sunshine was turning the leaves to gold. A few guests were already strolling beside the pool, just like any other morning. At least out here, all traces of the previous night's near disaster had vanished. "This looks wonderful, Melanie."

They moved aside as a bellboy carried more chairs from the restaurant and arranged them near the patio tables. "Everyone's been pitching in," Melanie said. "We're expecting a crowd."

"Oh, no. I should have warned you. I'm afraid a number of guests decided to leave early."

"I heard, but that's not the crowd I meant." Melanie smiled. "Renee's been busy, too. She contacted all the emergency personnel who were here last night and invited them to bring their families for breakfast."

Charlotte nodded in approval. Renee was the second oldest of the Marchand sisters, a successful Hollywood producer, but for the past few months she had thrown her experience and her talent for networking into handling the hotel's public relations. "That's a brilliant idea. They don't get enough thanks."

"That's exactly the angle Renee's using with her press release."

"She contacted the press? I would have thought we would want to minimize news of our difficulties."

"Her theory is that the story about the fire will make the papers anyway. The hotel might as well put a positive spin on it and use the free publicity."

"I see her point. This could work to our advantage."

"You didn't expect to handle this latest problem on your own, did you?"

If necessary, she would have—it was hard to break old habits—but Charlotte knew she still needed her sisters' help. Last fall, after their mother's unexpected heart attack had left Charlotte with more than she could handle, she'd swallowed her pride and asked all three of her sisters to combine their efforts with hers to run the hotel. Every day since then she was grateful that they'd agreed. The Hotel Marchand couldn't have stayed in business this long without them.

Yet she understood full well that the hotel didn't mean as much to them as it did to her. True, they had a sentimental attachment to it since they had all been raised within these walls. Yet if they lost it, they would have plenty left to fill their lives.

In the past month and a half, Melanie, Renee and the freespirited Sylvie had each fallen in love and were planning their weddings. Even their mother had announced she was going to remarry. It was astounding that despite the ongoing problems at the hotel, four of the Marchand women had managed to find the time for romance.

When was it going to be her *turn?*

Charlotte suppressed the thought and glanced around the courtyard, concentrating on doing a mental inventory of the available seating. She was happy for her mother and her sisters, she truly was. She'd learned the hard way she simply wasn't suited for marriage, so she wasn't going to dwell on her lack of romance. That would be almost as absurd as wishing for magic.

She'd tried that yesterday and all she'd gotten in reply had been a fire alarm.

"Who's that man talking to Mac near the pool?" Melanie asked, touching Charlotte's shoulder. "He's been watching you since we came outside."

"It's probably Detective Fergusson. I said I'd meet him when I got in this morning." Charlotte glanced toward the pool. "To be honest, I would have preferred to deal with Detective Rothberg, since I know he can be discreet. I don't want the customers disturbed any more than they already have been."

"Rothberg?"

"He was the one who investigated the death of that guest last month. Rothberg struck me as a very competent, professional man. I can only hope that Detective Fergusson will prove to be, as well…."

Her words trailed off as she caught sight of the man standing beside Mac. A tickle of warmth spread between her shoulder blades and down her spine. That wasn't the plump, mustachioed New Orleans cop who was investigating the fire, it was Jackson Bailey.

He was in almost the same spot where she'd first seen him yesterday, but this time there were no shadows or soot to mask his face. She'd known she would likely bump into him again— Mac had told her Jackson was a guest here, and as she'd learned when she'd checked the hotel register, he'd reserved his room for a week. Still, she had a cowardly urge to pretend that she hadn't noticed him. She already had enough to deal with; she didn't want to add more emotions to the mix.

But there was no way any woman could fail to notice a man like Jackson. It wasn't only his height or the broad shoulders that stretched out his black sweater. Nor was it the luxurious sable-brown hair that brushed the edges of his collar and fell haphazardly across his forehead in a way that begged for a woman's touch. It wasn't the easy grace of the way he stood in those cowboy boots either, with his weight shifted to one side and his hands hooked carelessly in his pockets. He had a presence about him, an energy that was as undeniable as the sunshine on the trees.

In high school he'd been called a beanpole, but no one would think of calling him that now. The denim jacket and faded jeans he'd worn yesterday had been replaced by pleated pants and a fine-knit turtleneck. It was obvious by the way his clothes fit that his body had filled out in all the right places. The gangliness of youth had become the classic contours of a man in his prime.

His physique wasn't the only thing that had changed with the years. The features that used to be too sharp for his face had been honed into ruggedness. Experiences she couldn't begin to guess at were etched into each line and angle. The overall effect would have been compelling even if he'd been a complete stranger.

It was no surprise she hadn't recognized him immediately last night, given the poor lighting and her state of mind. In this tall, self-assured man there was little trace left of the boy she'd once adored.

Except for his smile. That crooked tilt of his lips was still the same, even though the lines that bracketed his mouth were deeper.

And his eyes hadn't changed either. They were the same dusky blue, like the color of an August evening. He used to have a way of looking at her as if he'd noticed more than others did, seeing straight past the perfect girl she tried to be and loving her for the imperfect girl she was.

He broke off his conversation with Mac and started forward, his gaze locked on hers.

Melanie nudged her. "Is he your cop? He doesn't look like one."

"He's not my anything," Charlotte murmured. "That's Jackson Bailey."

"Jackson…" Melanie gasped and leaned her head closer to Charlotte's. "*Your* Jackson?"

"I told you, he's not *my* anything."

"Oh, my God! That can't be Jackson the beanpole. He's gorgeous!"

"You're engaged."

"That's got nothing to do with my eyesight. Why didn't you tell me he was back?"

"You were only nine when he left. I didn't think you'd remember him."

"Are you kidding? I had a huge crush on him."

"You what?"

"We all did. I was devastated when you dumped him for Adrian."

There was no time for Charlotte to think about that, let alone correct her. In a few long strides Jackson closed the remaining distance between them. The lines beside his mouth deepened in the hint of a smile. "Hello, Charlotte."

At least he hadn't called her Charlie again. That had taken her off guard yesterday. She hadn't been Charlie for twenty years. "Good morning, Jackson."

"Jackson Bailey!" Melanie said. "It really is you. What a nice surprise."

He shifted his gaze from Charlotte to her sister. "Hello."

Melanie stretched up to kiss his cheek. "Don't you recognize me? I'm Melanie."

He tilted his head to study her for a moment, a mannerism that stirred images from the past. He'd done that when he'd been younger, too. "The pest?" he asked.

Melanie grinned. "So you do remember."

"You were hard to forget." The smile that had been playing around the corners of his lips grew. "You look all grown up."

"Melanie's our sous-chef now," Charlotte said. "And she's engaged to our executive chef. They're both doing a fabulous job."

"I'm not surprised. I remember you were always hanging around your papa's kitchen." He winked at Melanie. "When you weren't trying to hang around us, that is. You had an uncanny knack for timing."

"Well, someone had to keep you and Charlotte from necking under the staircase."

Charlotte felt a blush seep into her cheeks. She strove to retain her composure, reminding herself that she was a forty-year-old woman, not a teenager in the throes of puppy love. "Don't you have a turkey to cook, Melanie?"

"Actually I do." She backed away. "It was good seeing you again, Jackson."

"You, too, pest."

"Even though it looks as if Charlotte's still trying to get rid of me?" She laughed and turned to leave. "Some things never change."

Charlotte waited until her sister had moved away, then smoothed an imaginary wrinkle from her suit and put on one of her most polite smiles. "I'm glad we ran into you this morning, Jackson."

He looked at her, lifting one eyebrow in silent skepticism as if he'd known she'd been considering ignoring him.

He couldn't still see through her, could he? It was a disconcerting thought. She laid two fingers lightly on his sleeve, determined to get the conversation under control. "We didn't have a chance to talk last night, but I wanted to tell you how sorry I was about what happened to your uncle."

His smile disappeared. Jackson's uncle, William Armstrong, had been shot while rescuing Anne Marchand during an attempted carjacking, and his heroism had almost cost him his life. "Thank you."

"Have you seen him yet?"

He nodded. "I went to the hospital straight from the airport."

"I understand he's making amazing progress."

"For a sixty-five-year-old man who had a bullet dug out of his lung three days ago, he's doing better than anyone could expect."

Charlotte suppressed a shudder. "We're all more grateful to him than words can say. Your uncle likely saved our mother's life. What he did was very brave."

"Anne said the police haven't made any progress in the case."

"No, she never got a good look at the carjacker. It all happened too fast."

"She seemed well when I saw her. But from what the nurses told me, she's barely left William's side."

"She feels responsible for what happened. He was coming to her aid when he was shot."

"There's more to her vigil than gratitude. They told me they're engaged."

"Yes."

He dipped his head, his gaze searching hers. "How do you feel about that?"

"I think it's wonderful," she said immediately. And she did, she reminded herself. Although she loved her father, he'd been dead for more than four years. William was a good man.

While Charlotte had been suspicious of his relationship with Anne at first, he'd proven his feelings for her mother were sincere. Above all, Anne was a warm, loving woman and she deserved a second chance at happiness.

"What about you?" she asked. "It doesn't bother you that William's remarrying, does it?"

"Why should it? He and Anne seem happy together and they have a lot in common." His arm flexed beneath her touch. "And I'd say they're old enough to know what they're doing."

Not like us, she added silently. She and Jackson had had nothing in common—they'd been a textbook example of opposites attracting. And they'd been too young to know how to do anything.

Well, that wasn't entirely true. There had been some things they'd eventually fumbled their way through despite their youth and their ignorance…

The heat in her cheeks deepened as Charlotte realized with a start that she was still touching him. She'd meant it as a polite but brief gesture, yet somehow her fingers had spread. Through the smooth fabric of his sleeve she could feel a ridge of lean muscle along his forearm.

His arm certainly hadn't felt like that twenty years ago.

She shifted, intending to pull away to prevent the moment from getting awkward, but before she could withdraw, he laid his hand over hers.

The contact of his skin with hers was electric. There was no other way to describe it. He didn't squeeze or hold her. The weight of his fingers—and the memories—kept her in place.

They used to hold hands a lot. It had been a chaste caress, but to two teenagers in love it had been something special.

Whether they'd been sitting in the bleachers cheering their team or riding the streetcar or walking home, they'd always been touching. She'd loved the way her small hand had fit in his large one. The simple touch had made her feel protected. Sometimes when he'd smiled a certain way, it had made her feel giddy.

Above all, it had made her feel cherished.

She moved her gaze to their joined hands. The long, supple fingers that covered her knuckles now weren't those of the boy she'd known. They belonged to a successful and well-respected surgeon.

Jackson had become a doctor, she reminded herself. Just as he'd always dreamed.

Then he'd left her behind so he could go off and save the world.

Something ugly stirred deep inside. It surprised her—she'd thought she'd buried that resentment a long time ago. At least the pain had faded to a distant ache. As she'd told Melanie, he wasn't *her* Jackson anymore.

Cutlery clanked near the tables where the buffet was being set up. Voices drifted on the breeze, mixing with the sound of birds and the rustling of leaves to bring Charlotte firmly back to the present. The warmth from the memories was snuffed out, finally allowing her to focus on what she was seeing.

A jagged red line cut through the sprinkling of dark hair on the back of Jackson's right hand.

"Mon Dieu," she murmured. "You didn't tell me you were injured, too."

"What?"

"In the fire. How—"

"No, that happened a while ago," he said, withdrawing his hand. "There was a bombing at the hospital in Kabul where I was working. I caught some shrapnel."

"How awful."

"It's a hazard of the job."

"Miss Marchand, we heard you had some trouble here yesterday."

At the voice, her shoulders stiffened. She had been so wrapped up in her conversation with Jackson she hadn't been aware that anyone had approached, yet she recognized Richard Corbin's cigarette-roughened drawl. Until now she'd only spoken with him on the phone. What on earth was he doing here now? She turned, not bothering to put on a pleasant expression.

Two men stood in front of her. The taller one met her gaze aggressively, yet it was his companion who made Charlotte uneasy—the way his flat gaze darted around the courtyard gave him the look of a vulture searching for his next meal.

Jackson moved closer to her side, positioning himself so his chest pressed gently against her shoulder. "Do you know these men, Charlotte?"

"We haven't met," she replied.

The shorter man nodded. "Not in person, but I believe Miss Marchand knows who we are. I'm Dan Corbin and this is my brother Richard."

"The Corbins are interested in buying the hotel," Charlotte said to Jackson. "My mother has repeatedly declined their offers."

"How is Mrs. Marchand?" Richard asked. "We heard she had some trouble, too."

"A carjacking, wasn't it?" Dan shook his head. "How unfortunate. Crime is everywhere these days."

"I hate to be rude, gentlemen," Charlotte said, "but I'm really very busy, so if you'll excuse me?"

"Since your mother hasn't been around lately, Miss Marchand, we'd like you to pass this on to her." Dan reached into his suit coat and withdrew a thick white envelope. Her mother's name was scrawled across the front in black ink. "This is a business proposition," he said, holding it out to Charlotte. "Under the circumstances, it should be of interest to all of you."

She crossed her arms. "As my mother already made clear, we have no business to discuss. The Hotel Marchand is not for sale."

"Don't be so hasty. These troubles you've been having at the hotel must be cutting into your profits." He tapped the envelope against her wrist. "You'd be smart to sell now. If you wait, the price might go down further."

Before Charlotte could respond, Jackson stepped forward, placing himself between her and the Corbins. "That sounded like a threat."

Dan had to tip his head back to meet Jackson's gaze. He paused for a moment, then replaced the envelope inside his suit and stepped back. "Not at all. It was merely some professional advice." He turned his flat gaze on Charlotte. "You have our number. Let us know when you change your mind."

They left after that, using the alley beside the bar rather than going through the French doors to the lobby. Charlotte remained where she was until they were out of sight. She had handled all manner of people in her years with the hotel, including bullies like these, and she was seldom disturbed by them. Still, she was more grateful for Jackson's solid presence than she wanted to admit.

The Corbin brothers had always been pushy, but their manner today had seemed openly belligerent, bordering on smug. Obviously they must have realized what a blow yesterday's fire had been to the hotel's business.

"Are you okay?" Jackson asked quietly.

No, she thought, she wasn't okay. The sunshine seemed too bright, the clink of dishes and background murmur of voices and birdsong seemed too loud. She'd believed she was getting on top of things, but encountering the Corbins had served to remind her how much remained to be done. "I need to get back to my office," she said, heading for the lobby doors.

He fell into step beside her, the solid thud of his boots blending with the tap of her heels. "Are the business offices still where your parents had them?"

"Yes."

"I'll walk you up."

"Thank you, but—"

"I think you should call the police, Charlotte." He slowed to let her enter the lobby ahead of him, then placed his palm on the small of her back as they wove their way past the potted plants and a pair of wing chairs. He didn't speak again until they started up the curving staircase. "That man threatened you."

"He didn't threaten me, he was only taking advantage of the situation as an attempt to intimidate me."

"I get the feeling it's more than that. The Corbins look like a couple of crooks."

That had been her first impression, as well, but she tried to be fair. "Both Mac and your uncle William checked them out after they made their first offer. Their manners may be unpleasant, but they appear to be legitimate businessmen. They have a chain of hotels in the Far East and are hoping to expand their operation in America."

Jackson fell silent as Charlotte paused at the top of the stairs to greet a few guests on their way to breakfast. She thought he would drop the subject, but as soon as they were out of earshot he continued where he'd left off. "One of the Corbins mentioned your profits. Is the hotel in financial trouble?"

This was something else about Jackson that hadn't changed, she thought. If he saw a need, he never hesitated to get involved in other people's problems. It was one of the qualities that she'd admired about him—he was forever defending the underdog.

Yet that very quality had also set him on the path that had taken him away.

Another echo of the old resentment stirred. Even as she acknowledged it, she reminded herself that it was unreasonable. They were no longer teenagers. They had both made choices and had moved on.

She stopped in the corridor outside her office and automatically tried for a professional smile, once more hoping to get the conversation under control. "The entire city has had its problems, and the Hotel Marchand is no exception. We've experienced some lean times, but we're recovering."

"Is that why you haven't been sleeping?"

"Excuse me?"

"You're covering it well, but I can see that you're exhausted."

"It's been a busy night. I'm fine."

He cupped her shoulders and regarded her closely. "Are you, Charlie?"

The urge to lean into him struck without warning. She wanted to step into his arms and fit her head to his shoulder just the way she used to. She longed to feel his warmth enfold her and his breath stir her hair. For one mad, rebellious instant she wanted to pretend she was his Charlie again, with no one depending on her and nothing to worry about except studying for the next midterm and trying to find the right prom dress.

She curled her nails into her palms and held herself rigid. What on earth was the matter with her? "I appreciate your concern, Jackson," she said. "But don't treat me like one of your causes."

"Whoa, where did that come from?"

"Sorry, I'm a bit stressed." She stepped aside to unlock her office door, using the motion to move away from his touch. "Give my regards to your uncle when you see him next. I'm sure you're anxious to get back to the hospital…."

Her words trailed off as she noticed a glimmer on the threshold. It was a cluster of tiny white sequins.

She pushed the door open and stepped inside. A white feather wafted in the breeze from the window. More sequins were scattered on the hardwood floor and gleamed beneath the carved pecan chairs that she kept for visitors.

"Charlotte, wait!" Jackson looped his arm around the front of her waist and pulled her back to his chest. "Don't touch anything."

The sudden contact with his body stole her breath and muddled her mind, making it hard to understand his warning. Sensations bombarded her. The muscle she'd felt beneath his sleeve was nothing compared to the firm strength she felt everywhere else. He definitely wasn't a boy any longer.

And her response to him wasn't that of an innocent girl. Her pulse pounded, knocking her senses into overdrive. Awareness that was purely sexual shot into every private region of her body.

She clenched her jaw, forcing herself to ignore the reaction. It had to be surprise mixed with fatigue. She concentrated on looking around. Apart from the sequins, the room appeared as clean and orderly as it always did.

But then her gaze reached the antique cherrywood table that served as her desk, and her knees gave out. She pressed into Jackson, welcoming his support.

Amidst a pile of white feathers, the shell of her beautiful, whimsical Mardi Gras mask lay in the center of her desktop. It was stripped naked of its trimmings and skewered to the wood by a knife.

CHAPTER THREE

JACKSON FOLDED HIS arms over his chest and leaned a shoulder against the door frame, watching as Detective Otis Fergusson jotted something in his notebook. If his white mustache were a beard, he'd look like Santa Claus checking his list. His weight alone wasn't responsible for the impression, it was his round face and jovial demeanor. Given the resemblance, Jackson wasn't sure why he didn't trust the man. Maybe for someone who worked in law enforcement he seemed too good-natured to be true.

Still, he appeared to be going through all the right motions, so he was probably competent enough.

Apart from the raw gouge that had been left in the wood, the surface of Charlotte's desk was clean. All traces of the savaged mask had been removed. Fergusson had pried the knife out of the desktop and bagged it as evidence, yet he wasn't hopeful it would lead anywhere. According to the detective, the weapon was a skinning knife, a favorite choice of poachers who worked the marshes and bayous. This one had been an inexpensive, run-of-the-mill variety, available in any sporting-goods store.

"I assure you, Detective, the door was locked when I arrived." Charlotte sat behind her desk and folded her hands primly on her lap. "The connecting door to my assistant's office was locked, as well."

Fergusson eased himself down on one of the chairs in front of the desk, propped his notebook on his crossed leg and waved his pen at the doors. "I don't mean to criticize, but those locks are on the flimsy side."

"Until now we've had no need for better ones."

"Do you have any idea who could have done this, Miss Marchand?"

Charlotte kept her face impassive as she glanced around the room. For someone who had obviously been up all night and had been fielding one problem after another for too long, she was holding herself together well. She had gone into what Jackson was starting to think of as her tea-in-the-parlor mode, doing her best to act composed, but he knew she wasn't as calm as she appeared. He'd felt the truth when she had trembled in his arms.

He was surprised how much he'd wanted to keep her there. Logically he knew he shouldn't get involved. She'd been right to deflect his questions earlier; the hotel was none of his business. She was a strong, competent woman. She didn't need him—she never had. She'd made that clear when she'd married Adrian Grant.

Yet somehow he couldn't bring himself to leave.

"I think you should talk to the Corbins, Detective," Jackson said.

Fergusson twisted to glance over his shoulder. "Corbins? Who are they?"

"Richard and Dan. They were in the hotel minutes before we found the knife."

Charlotte seemed about to protest, but then she dipped her chin in agreement. "I hate to cast suspicion on fellow hoteliers, but I must be realistic. The Corbin brothers are the only ones who stand to gain from an act of intimidation like this."

The detective's chair creaked loudly as he faced Charlotte once more. "Why would you think that, Miss Marchand?"

"They're hoping to buy this hotel. Perhaps they wanted to shake me up."

"Why would they leave a mask? Do you think that's some kind of message?"

"It could be. Every hotel in the city is counting on making a profit during this Mardi Gras period. Destroying the mask..." She paused. "It could be interpreted as significant. But whoever did this didn't bring the mask with them. It was already here."

"Oh?"

"It was part of my costume for our annual ball next week. The last time I saw it was yesterday evening just before the fire."

Fergusson tapped his pen against his notebook. "This has possibilities. I'll look into it."

"Thank you," she said. "For the sake of the hotel's reputation, I do hope you will be able to keep your investigation discreet. Our guests have come here to have a good time, and I want to make sure their stay is as pleasant as possible."

The detective's teeth gleamed beneath his mustache in a benign smile. "I'll do what I can to accommodate you, Miss Marchand. You people sure are having more than your share of problems lately."

"It seems that way, Detective. Have you made any progress regarding yesterday's fire?"

"We're still working on it," Fergusson said. "These things take time."

Charlotte leaned forward. "You mentioned the possibility of arson. Do you still feel that way?"

"At this point, it appears as if the cause could have been faulty wiring. But we're not ruling anything out." He pushed to his feet and turned to Jackson. "As a matter of fact, I was hoping to speak with you today, Dr. Bailey. I understand you were one of the first on the scene."

"That's right, but I can't tell you much about the fire. I was concentrating on treating the injured."

"You're only visiting New Orleans, is that right?"

"Yes. I divide my time between my NGO work overseas and my position with a hospital in Philadelphia."

He flipped back a few pages in his notebook. "What can you tell me about Luc Carter, the concierge?"

"I bandaged a wound on his arm."

"Yes, that's what I've heard. How did he seem to you?"

"I'm not sure what you're getting at."

"How was he acting? Did you notice anything suspicious?"

Charlotte looked at him from behind her desk, her gaze alert, as if she were waiting for his reply.

Jackson shook his head. "If you think he had something to do with it, you're wrong. He'd been trying to put out the fire with his jacket."

"Did you witness that?"

"No, but that's what he told me, and I had no reason to doubt his sincerity. He was obviously upset, and his jacket was charred black. And in spite of his own injury, he helped me give first aid to a burn victim."

Fergusson made a noncommittal noise, then closed his notebook and stored it in the pocket of his suit coat. "Thank you for your cooperation, Dr. Bailey. Miss Marchand, I'll be in touch."

Jackson pushed away from the door frame. "Wait. Aren't you going to give Charlotte any protection?"

"Sorry, sir. Not unless there's a confirmed threat to her person."

"Someone rammed a skinning knife into her desk. I might not have any expertise in law enforcement, but that looks like a personal threat to me."

"I can ask our regular patrols to keep an eye out for anything suspicious in the neighborhood," Fergusson said, walking to the door.

"It's Mardi Gras," Jackson said. "How would they spot anything suspicious in the crowds?"

"Sorry, with the department budget the way it is, that's all I can do."

Jackson had dealt with enough bureaucrats in his time to recognize a brick wall when he saw it. He waited until the detective was gone, then closed the door and turned to Charlotte.

"Jackson, it's all right," she said before he could speak. "I'll alert Mac to the situation and have him step up security."

"Mac told me that he's leaving, going back to his private security business."

"Yes, but not until after Mardi Gras. Our night security manager, Tyrell Haynes, will take over the job then. He's quite competent, and I have every confidence in him."

"Are you sure that stepping up the security here will be

enough? The design of this hotel makes it impossible to keep anyone out."

"It will be fine."

"There are too many entrances. You saw how easily the Corbins walked in this morning."

"This vandalism could still prove to be nothing but a sick prank. Yet if the Corbins are indeed responsible, they would want me to panic. That's why I can't afford to overreact."

"But—"

"I'm not going to lock the place down during Mardi Gras, Jackson. Nor do I want to alarm the guests with a police presence. Other than stepping up our in-house security, my only option is business as usual." She ran a fingertip over the scar in the desktop, then rose to her feet. "And I would ask that you don't mention this incident to your uncle."

"Why not?"

"My mother has enough worries already, and this ugliness will only upset her further. With her heart condition, I don't want to take any chances."

"You can't expect me to forget about this."

"That's exactly what I expect. While I appreciate your concern, I'll handle things from here. As you just said, you don't have any expertise in law enforcement. And, to be blunt, this isn't any of your business."

Frustrated, he raked his fingers through his hair. He knew she was right—he'd already told himself he didn't want to get involved—but hearing her say it bothered him. "You told Mac we're old friends."

"It's true. We were friends once, regardless of the way we parted."

"Then as a friend I have the right to be concerned."

"Perhaps, but not to pry."

"If my uncle marries your mother, we're going to be family."

"Which is why I've tried to be courteous. But this is my problem, not yours. You're leaving soon anyway, aren't you? Running off to Afghanistan or wherever?"

The bitterness in her voice startled him. This was the first crack in her calm she'd allowed since they'd arrived at her office. "If everything goes well, yes," he replied. "I'm still needed there."

She tugged the hem of her jacket to straighten it and moved around her desk. "Then since your visit here is only temporary, there's no reason for you to get involved in my problems."

"Charlotte—"

"I realize there was a time when I asked you to stay, but believe it or not, I've managed fine without you."

"I can see you have. I'm only trying to help."

"Running one small family hotel wasn't noble or exciting enough for you twenty years ago. You had no trouble keeping out of my life then, so I'm sure it won't be that difficult to stay out of it now."

There were countless things Jackson could say in return. He had plenty of accusations he could toss out, as well as pain of his own to remember. He'd kept out of her life because she'd pushed him out. There wouldn't have been room for both him and her new husband.

Yet this was ancient history, he reminded himself, and he hadn't come here to change the past. Charlotte's reaction was out of proportion to the circumstances. Combined with the exhaustion he had noticed earlier, she was exhibiting the symptoms of someone under extreme stress. His concern for her deepened. "What's going on here, Charlotte?"

She brushed past him and jerked the door open. "Good-bye, Jackson."

He reached around her and shoved the door closed with his palm.

She held herself motionless for a good ten seconds, her mouth compressed into a tight line. Then she tipped back her head and glared at him. Her eyes shone with a confused mix of emotions, and anger was the least of them.

Charlotte's calm wasn't merely cracked, Jackson thought, it had shattered and fallen away like the mangled Mardi Gras mask.

Damn, he wanted to hold her again. But if he touched her now, it wouldn't be as a friend or as a potential cousin-in-law. He would be responding to a reflexive male urge to hold an attractive woman. Neither of them needed a complication like that. He took a steadying breath and kept his arms at his sides. "All this passion isn't really about us, is it?"

"What?"

"As much as it would stroke my ego to think you've been pining for me for the last twenty years, I don't believe that's true."

"Of course it isn't true."

"Well, then, if the passion isn't about us, it has to be the hotel, right?"

Tears brimmed in her eyes. "I was doing fine until you showed up."

"No, you weren't or you wouldn't be this close to the edge. But I get the feeling that I'm the last straw."

"Yes, damn you!"

"Why?"

"How dare you act concerned about my difficulties when the truth is you'd be happy to see the hotel fail?"

"That's ridiculous."

"No, it isn't." She pressed her index finger to his chest. "You hate this place. That's what you said the last time I saw you."

She was right; he had said that. "I was angry. You know I didn't mean it."

"No? You certainly were in a hurry to go on your one-man crusade to save the world." She tapped him with her nail. "How lucky for you that you came back now. You're just in time to gloat."

He tried to restrain himself from responding in kind, but it was tough. The argument was an old one, and they'd never really finished it. "Charlie—"

"Don't call me that!" She walked back to her desk, her normally graceful strides hard and choppy.

He rubbed his jaw. "Are things really that bad? Could the hotel fail?"

"We have no more financial reserves. We're mortgaged to the limit. If we don't turn a profit by next week—" She halted suddenly and stooped to pick up something from the floor. It was a tiny, white feather.

Her shoulders trembled, as if the sight of that feather crumbled the final layer of her control. She closed it in her fist and turned to face him. "I've made this hotel my life, Jackson. It's all I have. The possibility of losing it…" Her voice broke. The tears she'd been struggling to hold back trickled down her cheeks.

She must have been bottling this up for weeks, Jackson

thought. It probably did her good to let it out, so he wasn't going to try to stop her. But the urge to hold her was nearly overpowering...

The significance of what she'd just said struck him all at once. *She could lose the hotel.*

The irony was almost too much to believe. After all these years, what were the chances the same thing would be happening to both of them? "I understand what you're going through, Charlotte," he said.

She swiped her knuckles under her eyes. "No, I don't think you could. You followed your dream. You always lived your life how you wanted to. No one can take that away from you."

"You're wrong. I know exactly what it's like to watch everything you've built, everything you are, slip out of your grasp."

"How could you?"

He lifted his right hand, palm out. "Do you know how many nerves there are in the human hand? How many muscles, bones and tendons?"

"I have no idea. Why?"

Still holding up his hand, he walked toward her. "Look carefully." He spread his fingers until the throbbing warned him to stop. "You already saw the back. Take a good look at the rest. This is where the shrapnel went in."

She blinked, her gaze going to his mutilated palm. It took her a moment to focus on the mass of red gouges and puckered ridges that crisscrossed the center. When she did, the color drained from her cheeks. She stepped closer and grasped his fingers. "Oh, dear God, Jackson," she murmured. "The wound goes all the way through."

"Human flesh is no match for shredded metal traveling at a hundred feet a second."

"I hadn't realized the injury was this serious."

"I was one of the lucky ones. It was only my hand, so I lived."

"It looks as if it's healing."

"On the outside, yes."

She clasped his hand gingerly between both of hers and looked up at him. "And on the inside? How bad is it?"

"I can't hold a scalpel. I can't even tie a damn bandage."

Fresh tears glistened on her lashes. "Oh, no."

"*This* is why I came home. I'm going to see a friend of mine at Tulane for tests that will determine whether the damage to my hand can be repaired. I had my flight booked before William was shot."

"Jackson, I'm so sorry."

"I don't want your pity, Charlotte. I just want you to know that I'm the last person who would gloat over your troubles." He pulled free from her touch and dropped his arm to his side. "And it looks as if we've both got plenty of those. We sure as hell don't need to stir up the ones from our past."

CHARLOTTE WALKED slowly along the perimeter of the room, running her fingers over the gracefully arching leaves of a potted fern. Music seeped in through the tall windows that faced the street—celebrations in the Quarter were going into full swing—yet apart from the click of her heels on the wood floor, this event room was silent tonight. The wedding reception that had been scheduled here had been canceled at the last minute after the wedding was called off. The emptiness should have bothered her because it meant lost revenue that

was sorely needed. Instead she was grateful for some time to be alone with her thoughts.

She wasn't sure how she'd gotten through the day. Somehow she'd managed to put on a good front to keep the staff motivated and the remaining guests happy. She'd even made a stab at going through the checklist for the gala Mardi Gras ball that would take place in this room next Tuesday.

And all the while she'd been haunted by the image of the mangled, scarcely healed flesh on Jackson's palm.

How on earth could she have vented her frustration with her own situation on him? Granted, she'd had one bitch of a day, and seeing Jackson again had definitely pushed all her buttons, yet her behavior had been inexcusable. Even though the haze of emotion that had driven her had burned out within minutes, the echoes of what she'd said had lingered like the acrid, smoky aftertaste from yesterday's fire.

Given his own circumstances, he'd shown incredible restraint. That was something new—the boy she'd known had been as open with his feelings as she used to be. Still, the compassion in his gaze hadn't changed.

Neither had that uncanny ability he possessed to see straight through her.

She stopped beside the bay window that arched outward from the corner of the room and smoothed her palm along the plush window seat. Would Jackson be able to feel this velvet? Would he be able to enjoy the simple pleasure of fern leaves sliding through his fingers?

Truthfully she couldn't imagine Jackson Bailey as anything but a doctor. She'd resented his choice when he'd made it because she'd had a different vision for their future. With the idealistic—and stubbornly blinkered—thinking of youth, she'd dreamed of following in the footsteps of the parents she'd idolized. Because of that, she'd hoped someday to run this hotel with Jackson and raise their own family where she had grown up. For a while it had seemed her wish would come true.

But then Jackson had won a scholarship that had allowed him to pursue his own dream. He'd been right to do it. It hadn't been ambition that had driven him to become a surgeon, it had been a genuine need to make a difference. Rather than devoting himself to only one family, he'd saved the lives of countless others.

And so Jackson had made practicing medicine his life, just as Charlotte had made the hotel hers. They had gone their separate ways, yet after two decades apart, somehow they had arrived at the same point. They both were facing the possibility of losing the very things they'd dedicated their lives to....

The very things they'd chosen over each other.

It was ironic that they would meet again now. If there was such a thing as fate, it must have a twisted sense of humor.

"Auntie Charlotte!"

She turned toward the door in time to see a small figure barrel through. She shook off her dark mood, her mouth moving into the first genuine smile she'd felt for hours. "Daisy Rose," she said, holding out her arms. "How's my favorite niece?"

Daisy Rose raced across the gleaming floor, her long curly hair streaming behind her like red pennants. She skidded the last few feet before she collided with Charlotte's legs, then clasped her arms around her aunt's knees and leaned back. "I've got wings."

"Well, of course you do," Charlotte said, stroking her niece's hair back from her face. "You're our little angel."

"No, *real* wings." She wiggled her shoulders. "Look!"

Charlotte leaned over to check. Sure enough, a pair of wings fashioned from wire and white tulle hung crookedly from Daisy's shoulders. "They're lovely!"

"Watch me fly." She bounced on her toes, craning her neck in order to peer over her shoulder. "See?"

The wire-and-tulle contraption flapped and wobbled sideways. Charlotte carefully adjusted it back into place. "That's wonderful."

"I'm a fairy." She spun away from Charlotte, waving the stick in her hand. A gold-painted foam star tipped the end. "This is my wand, just like in the stories."

"Yes, *chère*. Just like the fairy tales."

She skipped back across the floor. "Mommy, look, I'm casting a spell."

Charlotte returned her gaze to the doorway. Sylvie Marchand entered the room in a dramatic billow of tie-dyed magenta silk. The resemblance between mother and daughter was unmistakable—they both had the same red hair as well as the same irrepressible zest. Sylvie paused only long enough to straighten Daisy's wings again, then swept over to Charlotte. "We're still working on the rest of the costume, but she couldn't wait to show you."

"It's going to be lovely," Charlotte said.

"She's over the moon about being able to stay up late. It's going to be her first Mardi Gras ball."

"That's the main reason Mama and I decided to break with tradition and go with the fairy-tale theme." Charlotte watched as Daisy moved around the room to tap each of the ferns with her wand. "Daisy has a vivid imagination."

"She adores those stories you read to her."

"So did I when I was her age. I'm sure she'll have a wonderful time."

Sylvie laughed. "She'll probably play herself out after the first half hour and sleep through the rest of it."

"That's what Melanie did at her first ball. Do you remember?"

"You're right." She propped her hands on her hips and looked past Charlotte. "We found her curled up like a kitten on that window seat."

"It seems like only yesterday."

"And speaking of first times…" Sylvie lowered her voice. "I heard Jackson Bailey's back in town."

Charlotte sighed. She should have realized word of Jackson's return would have spread. "Yes."

Sylvie wiggled her eyebrows suggestively. "I also heard he's improved with age."

"Men are lucky that way. Women simply age. How are things at the gallery?" she asked, trying to change the subject. Sylvie had taken over the management of the art gallery that was attached to the hotel. Like her sisters, she was using her own special talents to help keep the hotel afloat.

"Wonderful. I stopped by your office to give you an update earlier, but I didn't want to intrude."

"When? You know I always have time for you."

"From the sound of things, you and the new, improved edition of Jackson the beanpole were going at it already." Sylvie pursed her generous lips in a moue. "It's funny… Come to think of it, I haven't heard you raise your voice like that since he left."

Charlotte pressed her fingertips to her temples. "You heard?"

"I couldn't make out the words, but the passion came through loud and clear."

"It wasn't passion, it was stress."

"Mmm. I'd say there's still something there."

The denial Charlotte wanted to make didn't come as readily as she would have liked. She hadn't been pining for Jackson, yet she hadn't been able to think about much else all day. And what about that blast of sexual awareness that had taken her by surprise when he'd held her? She decided not to probe at that. Her feelings concerning Jackson were muddled enough already. "Is it true that you had a crush on him?"

Sylvie's eyes widened. "We were sworn to secrecy. Who told you? Was it Melanie?"

"She said you all did."

"It was inevitable. You know how we looked up to our big sister. And he was your beau, so he had to be fabulous. With those sensitive blue eyes and his rebel hair and the way he could make us smile…" She clasped her hands to her breasts and sighed theatrically. "He was so romantic."

"He was, wasn't he?"

Sylvie chuckled. "And to top it off, the Queen couldn't abide Jackson, so naturally that made him seem all the more romantic."

The Queen. Sylvie was referring to their grandmother, Celeste Robichaux, who had made no secret of her disappointment over Charlotte's interest in "that Bailey boy," as she'd called him.

It had been an ongoing though subtly waged battle. Celeste was old-guard Creole and she was proud of her family's history and their position among the cream of New Orleans society. She had insisted that, as her oldest granddaughter, Charlotte had a duty to choose someone who came with both old money and an impeccable pedigree.

Jackson had possessed neither. His father had repaired appliances for a living until he'd opened a store of his own. His mother had been the illegitimate product of a scandalous affair between a jazz pianist and Bennett Armstrong, one of the pillars of Celeste's society. Although Bennett's legitimate child, William Armstrong, had accepted his half sister and his nephew, Jackson, the rest of the Armstrong family had steadfastly refused to acknowledge their existence. None of that had mattered in the least to Charlotte, but her grandmother hadn't been able to look past it.

Celeste had approved of Adrian. She'd been the one to introduce him to Charlotte and she'd been so delighted at their wedding reception that she'd actually waltzed in this very room.

It had been Mardi Gras then, too.

Charlotte could only hope that this year's Mardi Gras wouldn't be the occasion for another disaster.

"Mama! Auntie Charlotte!"

Charlotte pulled herself from her musings to see Daisy whirling in circles toward them, one arm flung out from her side, still clutching her make-believe wand.

"I thought you were a fairy, *chère*, not a helicopter," Sylvie said.

"Look at my wand," she cried.

Charlotte stared at the gold star on the end of the stick. It was a trick of the lighting—or perhaps a side effect of the moisture that had sprung to her eyes—but a trail of gold appeared to stream from the tip.

"Make a wish, Auntie Charlotte," Daisy said, waving her wand as she passed. "It's magic!"

Magic? *Oh, no,* Charlotte thought. Even in a game, she wasn't going to risk asking for that again.

CHAPTER FOUR

"Do you know why they say doctors make the worst patients, Jacques?"

"Because we never pay?"

"It's because you insist on diagnosing and treating yourselves." Dr. Yves Fortier jabbed his finger at one of the X-rays that was clipped to the lighted display board beside him. "I told you to use the hand within reason. What have you been doing since you got to town? Delivering refrigerators for your papa's store?"

"I couldn't have if I'd wanted to," Jackson replied. "He moved the business to Des Moines after the last hurricane." He peered at the film. He couldn't spot any difference from the set of X-rays that had been among the diagnostic scans he'd had couriered to Yves last week. "Don't try to scare me, Yves. The hand's no worse."

"It should have been better." He moved his fingertip to the outline of one of the bones that had been chipped by the shrapnel. "I would have expected this to show some sign of absorption, but it's still intact."

"That bone isn't the issue. It won't impair any movement."

"It will if there are other fragments left that have blocked the nerve pathways. You should have come to me for the initial work. Whoever did this must have used a poker and barbecue tongs."

"There wasn't much left of the hospital after the bombing. You know how it is, Yves."

"Only too well. I shall need to ask Marie to fix you a gris-gris to counteract this butchery."

Jackson restrained himself from rolling his eyes. Yves' wife, Marie, was a fully qualified surgical nurse, but she was also a little eccentric, occasionally supplementing medicine with voodoo. It was a harmless hobby, and for some people it even provided comfort, so Jackson humored her when he could. "Will the charm cost me extra?"

"I thought you never paid, my friend." He studied the X-ray for another minute, then stepped back. "Okay, enough wasting of my valuable time with chitchat. Let's see how badly you've mucked yourself up."

The small room that served as Yves' combination examining room and research lab was tucked into a corner of the top floor of Tulane University's medical arts building like an afterthought, although this private lab was the primary reason the university had been able to coax him into joining their staff. Every available inch of space along the walls was crammed with shelves full of books, journals and electronic equipment—if there had ever been windows, they'd long ago become buried. Yves led the way to the only clear surface— a stainless-steel worktable in the center of the floor—and rolled a stool in front of it.

In spite of his gruff manner, he was gentle as he positioned Jackson on the stool, switched on the high-intensity light and centered a magnifying lens over his hand. He inspected the back patiently, taking careful notes and measurements of the position and the extent of the damage. It took three times as long for him to go through the same process with the palm.

Compared to the examinations Jackson had already undergone, Yves' initial approach was markedly low-tech, an odd choice for one of the world's leading neurosurgeons, but it was all part of his gift. He'd always maintained that science worked best when it was wielded with the heart as well as the brain.

Jackson had first met Yves and Marie in an Eritrean refugee camp. There hadn't been any MRIs or EEGs or ultrasound machines within a hundred miles—the beat-up generator outside the hospital tent had been barely able to power the lights. In spite of that, the Fortiers had labored six hours straight to save a ten-year-old girl whose leg had been almost severed at the hip by a machete.

The effort hadn't been reasonable, since the chances of success under those primitive conditions had been next to nil. Nevertheless, neither Yves nor Marie given up. As Marie had tirelessly worked the ventilator and shooed the flies off their patient with a switch made of goat hair, Yves operated by instinct and feel. Against all odds, by the following morning the girl had not only sat up but wiggled her toes.

"Next time put on a catcher's mitt," Yves muttered.

"What?"

"From the looks of this," he said, touching the eraser end of his pencil to the center of the scarring, "you tried to play catch with the shrapnel."

"Yeah, something like that."

Yves glanced up, his gaze keen. "How close to the blast were you?"

"The details are fuzzy."

"Perhaps that is a mercy."

Jackson nodded. "We've all seen things we would prefer to forget, Yves."

Yves grunted an agreement and let the subject drop. Like everyone who had worked in a war zone, he knew when not to push. He returned his attention to Jackson's hand. "How much sensation have you recovered?"

Jackson pointed to the base of his thumb. "This area is around thirty percent. This is maybe forty." He moved his index finger. "The rest is about sixty. Enough for basic grasping and holding but no fine motor control."

Yves switched off the light and swung the magnifying lens aside. "Huh, you've really done it this time, Jacques. You're well and truly mucked up."

"I know you can't resist a challenge."

"Do you think I have nothing better to do?"

"Since when did you become modest, Yves? We all know you're a genius."

"This is true. I am a genius." He slapped Jackson's shoulder. "Come back in two days and I'll hook up the electronic gizmos. We'll measure the nerve impulses and map out how much you left me to work with."

"Thanks, Yves."

"Don't thank me yet, my friend. This is only the first step."

Jackson recognized the caution in Yves' voice. He'd used the same tone himself when he'd been unsure of a patient's prognosis. Like Yves, he knew the odds of a full recovery were against him. But there was no way he could allow himself to give up.

Without his work, what would he have left?

The image of Charlotte stole into his mind. Not the silk-and-pearls Charlotte but the woman who had yelled at him yesterday, then had looked at his palm with tears on her lashes.

They hadn't seen each other since then, so why couldn't he stop thinking about her?

Jackson rubbed his face briskly and followed Yves to the door. Since he'd come home, there seemed to be no end to the questions he didn't know how to answer.

"EXCUSE ME, CHARLOTTE. Do you have a minute?"

Charlotte slowed her progress across the lobby as she saw Luc Carter step around the concierge desk and hurry toward her. She wanted nothing more than to keep walking until she reached her car, then drive home and have a two-hour bath and a ten-hour sleep, but it appeared that wasn't going to happen. She paused beside the furniture grouping closest to the front entrance and set her briefcase on a wicker chair. "Certainly, Luc. What can I do for you?"

He adjusted the knot of his tie and smoothed his hair. "I need to talk to you about the fire."

She regarded him curiously—the nervous fidgeting with his appearance was unusual for Luc. It would make a person think he had a guilty conscience. Her gaze was caught by the edge of the bandage that poked out from the cuff of his shirt, and she felt a quick jab of guilt herself.

Before Jackson had stated with such certainty that Luc had been putting out the fire, she'd actually considered the possibility that he'd been involved in setting it. The problems that had been plaguing the hotel had begun a few months after

Luc had come to work here. Charlotte's assistant had gone as far as suggesting that Luc was deliberately causing trouble so that he could make himself look good when he helped solve the problems. Yet hotel security had investigated him and hadn't found anything untoward. And Charlotte trusted Jackson's take on the situation—he'd always been a good judge of people.

She really hadn't wanted to suspect Luc of trying to hurt the business. He was an excellent concierge as well as a pleasant and charming young man. He was terrific with Daisy Rose, too, and Charlotte's mother and sisters had grown quite fond of him. It would have upset them if it had turned out that their faith in him was misplaced.

She touched her fingertips to his sleeve above the bandage. "Is this injury bothering you? If you want to take some time off, I'll understand."

"No, I can't even feel it. I don't need time off, it's the other way around."

"What do you mean?"

"I realize we lost customers because of the fire. I'd like to offer a portion of my wages as a way to help out."

Startled, she dropped her hand. "That's very generous of you, Luc."

"It's the least I can do, Charlotte. I know I haven't been here long, but you've all been so nice to me…." He cleared his throat. "You've treated me like part of the family."

She smiled. Many of the hotel's employees had expressed the same sentiment. It was one of the factors that had allowed the business to flourish as long as it had. "I'm happy you think so."

"I didn't expect it to happen when I took this job, but I feel as if I've finally found where I belong. You and your sisters and Miss Anne have taught me a lot about loyalty."

"That's good. We—"

"I never had any sisters or cousins around when I was growing up," he said, his tone growing more urgent. "But if I had, I know I would have wanted to protect them."

"Protect?" Her smile wavered. "Luc, what are you trying to say?"

The bell that sat on the concierge's desk chimed softly. A stocky gray-haired man was standing in front of it, his fingers drumming impatiently on the wood as he looked around the lobby.

Luc glanced at the customer and cursed under his breath. "I promise I'm going to do my best to watch out for all of you," he said firmly. "But, please, you need to be careful."

Had he heard about the knife in her desk? she wondered. She'd done her best to keep that quiet, but it was possible word of the vandalism had spread. "Let's talk in my office," she said, reaching for her briefcase. "You appear to have more on your mind."

The bell chimed again. Luc's cheek pulsed as if he were clenching his teeth. "I would like very much to talk with you, Charlotte, but it will have to wait. I have too much to do first. I'm sorry."

Concerned, she watched him return to his post to deal with the customer. The stocky man started speaking as soon as Luc reached him. They were too far away for her to discern the conversation, but from the expression on Luc's face, it couldn't be good. She tucked her briefcase under her arm and started across the lobby, intending to lend her assistance before they lost another guest.

The next thing she knew, she collided with a very solid, very male body. Her briefcase went flying as she brought her hands up to steady herself.

"Hey, are you okay?"

Even before she heard the voice she recognized who this was. The contact muddled her thoughts, just as it had the last time. And despite where they were and what was happening, the same mindless reaction raced through her body. Her pulse leaped, her breathing sped up and her senses filled with the tantalizing scent of warm male skin. "Jackson," she murmured. "Please excuse me. I wasn't watching where I was going."

He clasped her elbow. "I don't mind. Are you on your way in or out?"

She struggled to think. "Neither. I was going to help..." She glanced past his shoulder. Luc and the guest he'd been talking to were nowhere in sight. Whatever the problem had been, it appeared Luc was handling it.

She shifted her focus to Jackson's chest. He was wearing his beat-up denim jacket again, and somehow her hands had slipped through the open front and splayed on his shirt. A pleasant warmth tingled through her palms as she felt his chest rise and fall with his breathing. The top few buttons of his shirt were unfastened, baring the base of his throat. Along with the scent of his skin she caught the clean tang of the hotel's soap.

"Charlotte?"

She dropped her hands quickly, realizing he was still waiting for her reply. "Well, it looks as if I'm on my way out."

He bent over to retrieve her briefcase. "Are you through for the day?"

"If I can manage to get out the door without mowing down anyone else."

"I thought you lived here. Doesn't your family still have that apartment over the bar?"

"It got downsized in the last renovation, so my mother lives there on her own now. I have a place in Faubourg Marigny," she said, holding out her hand for her briefcase.

Instead of giving it to her, he used it to gesture toward the front entrance. "I'm on my way out, too. I'll walk you to your car."

She hesitated. "Thanks for your offer, but it isn't necessary, Jackson."

"I'm not planning to argue about the security issue with you again, if that's what you're worried about. Mac told me he and Tyrell stepped up surveillance of the hotel."

"Oh?"

"I just want to talk to you, that's all. We got off on the wrong foot yesterday and I'd like to remedy that, so if you're not busy…" He paused. "Or do you have a date?"

The absurdity of the question almost made her laugh. She? Have a date? She hadn't made the time to go out with anyone in longer than she cared to remember.

Could that be the reason she was having such a strong physical reaction to Jackson? Extended celibacy, along with stress and fatigue? That didn't make sense—celibacy had never bothered her before. She shook her head and finally met his gaze.

It jarred her to see the blue eyes of the teenager she'd known so well looking at her from the face of a man. His hair was endearingly tousled as usual, one lock stubbornly dipping across his forehead as if he'd combed it with his fingers. A hint of beard stubble darkened his jaw, making the lines beside his mouth and the hollows beneath his cheekbones appear even more masculine. How did he manage to look boyish and rugged at the same time?

Only a few minutes ago she'd been eager for a bath and her bed, but the thought of being alone no longer appealed to her. "Actually I've been hoping to get a chance to talk to you, too," she said, moving toward the door. "The way we left things yesterday was…"

"Damn awkward," he finished for her.

She couldn't disagree with that, she thought, stepping outside.

After the sedate graciousness of the hotel's interior, entering the street was a shock to the senses. The night was alive with movement and laughter. A woman in a spangled dress hawked Mardi Gras masks that had been stacked on a stick. Horse hooves clacked against the pavement as a calèche full of tourists rattled past a long black limousine. Buskers performed to clusters of onlookers, and a cacophony of music from at least four different sources echoed off the old buildings. Enveloping it all, the scents of fried shrimp and spilled beer drifted on the breeze, along with the underlying tang of the river.

Jackson inhaled slowly, his eyes half closing. "This is just how I remember it."

She knew immediately what he was talking about. "I know what you mean. There's nothing quite like the atmosphere of Mardi Gras."

"Yeah, I'm glad I get the chance to soak it in while I'm here. You're lucky, you see it every year."

"As strange as it sounds, I don't normally get the time to enjoy it. It's mainly business for me."

"It used to be the busiest time for the hotel when your parents ran things, too," he said.

"I hadn't realized how hard they worked back then. What I remember most were the colors. And all the movement. It seemed as if everything was in perpetual motion."

"And the music." He tilted his head as if to follow one melody in the mix. "The city was always full of music, but this time of year it explodes with it."

Of course he'd remember that, she thought. Musical talent ran in his family; Jackson had inherited his love of music from his scandalous grandmother. He'd also inherited her long, supple fingers. And like his grandmother, he had chosen a career that had taken full advantage of those marvelous hands...

He was carrying her briefcase in his left hand, Charlotte realized. She looked at his right. He held it loosely by his side. The dark line on the back was barely noticeable in this light, yet now that she knew what to look for, she could see that there was something odd about the slack angle of his thumb.

"Go ahead and ask if you want," he said.

She glanced up to find him watching her. "I'm sorry, I didn't mean to stare."

"It's okay, Charlotte. I'm not used to my limitations yet either, so I don't expect you to be." He pressed closer to her side as a group of people brushed past them. "We never tiptoed around each other before. I can't see any reason to start now."

He was right. They'd always been honest—they hadn't known any better. "Is it all right to move your hand around like that?" she asked. "Shouldn't you be wearing a sling or some kind of support?"

"Not at this stage. It will have to be completely immobilized after surgery, though."

"Does it...hurt?"

"The upside of nerve damage is that I don't feel much."

"I would like to say I'm glad for that, but I'm not glad about any of it, Jackson. It's just not fair."

"I gave up expecting fair a long time ago. One of the first things I learned with my NGO work is that fate doesn't play favorites."

There seemed nothing more to add to that, so they started walking toward the lot where Charlotte had parked. "Have you seen your friend at Tulane yet?" she asked.

He nodded. "He's going to do some more tests the day after tomorrow to gauge how much healing has taken place on its own."

"*Could* it heal on its own?"

"Not anymore." He sidestepped a pair of giggling young women who were weighed down with ropes of beads over their breasts. "That's why I waited as long as I did to get treatment," he said. "With an injury like this, it's best to give the nerves a chance to regenerate. Everything that could already did."

"Surgery could repair it, right?"

"I have to believe that, Charlotte."

Although he spoke softly, his voice was threaded with steel. It was a stark contrast to the merriment that whirled around them.

"But Yves is too smart to make promises," Jackson continued. "His initial diagnosis is that I mucked myself up good. He's considering prescribing a gris-gris."

"He sounds like a character."

"He is that, but he's also a brilliant doctor. His research into nanotechnology and laparoscopic neurosurgery is cutting-edge stuff." He glanced at her sideways. "No pun intended."

She knew he'd meant to make her smile, but she couldn't, not about this. "I hope everything works out for you, Jackson. You know that, don't you?"

"I know. Same goes for me. I hope you work through your troubles, too."

They drew near the nightclub at the end of the block. The wail of a saxophone spilled through the open doorway, adding yet another layer to the melody of the street. Charlotte waited until they had passed and the noise had faded before she spoke again. "I want to apologize for my behavior yesterday," she said. "It was inexcusable for me to be so touchy about the hotel."

"I'm glad you were. Otherwise you might still be trying to treat me like a stranger."

Put like that, she couldn't regret what she'd said, either. It felt good to be able to talk to Jackson like this again. "Well, I am sorry," she persisted. "You were only trying to be my friend."

"Stop apologizing. I do tend to stick my nose in where it's not wanted," he said wryly. "And speaking of that, I'm guessing that your family doesn't know how bad things are with the hotel finances. Otherwise you wouldn't have been bottling things up that way."

"You guessed right. They know our finances are precarious, but they don't know how close we are to losing the hotel. I've been shielding them from the full extent of the problems."

"Because of Anne's heart condition?"

"That's the main reason, yes."

"And because the hotel means more to you than it does to the others."

She closed her hand into a fist and gave his chest a light thump. "I can't believe you still know me so well. It's been two decades."

He paused under the streetlight on the corner and tipped up her chin with his knuckle. His gaze moved slowly over her face. "I know who you used to be, but I'm not sure about this person you are now."

"Have I changed that much?"

"Some. When did you start straightening your hair?"

"My hair? I'm surprised you noticed."

Still using his knuckle, he brushed a lock of hair from her cheek. "I remember winding your curls around my fingers." One side of his mouth lifted in a half smile. "I also remember getting your hair tangled in my watchband one night when you were trying to sneak past your papa."

She gave a startled laugh and touched his arm. "Oh, I remember that. I was so late I thought I'd be grounded for life if I got caught. You wanted to break your watch apart so I wouldn't cut my hair."

"Your hair was so beautiful, I couldn't let you lop it off."

"And I couldn't let you break that watch. You won it at the science fair."

"So you ended up tucking my watch into your curls and wearing it to bed."

"It worked. I didn't get grounded, but I had a heck of a time combing that watch out in the morning. Thank goodness Renee helped."

He smoothed his palm along her hair. "So when did you get rid of the curls?"

"Oh, ages ago. I think it was before my divorce."

His smile dimmed.

What was it about Jackson that made her speak without thinking? Charlotte looked at her hand where it still rested against his arm. And why did she always seem to end up touching him?

A group of people staggered past them from the direction of the nightclub, their voices raised in slurred conversation. Someone stumbled into her shoulder, giving her a good excuse to start moving again.

Jackson remained silent until they had rounded the corner and were within sight of the parking lot. "I should probably tell you I'm sorry things didn't work out for you and Adrian," he said.

"It's all right," she began.

"But I won't say that because I've never lied to you, Charlotte. I didn't like Adrian."

"You hardly knew him."

"I didn't move in the same circles as he did, but I recognized his type."

It had taken Charlotte five excruciating years to recognize what type Adrian Grant really was and another three before she'd finally divorced him. Her stubbornness hadn't been due to loyalty to the man she'd married, it had been from an unwillingness to let go of her dreams and face reality.

Still, she'd never spoken about Adrian to anyone. It was too humiliating. "At the risk of making things awkward again," she said, "I'd rather not discuss my marriage or my ex-husband with you."

"No problem. It's not a topic I would enjoy either. But while we're on the subject of the past, there's something I want to clear up."

"Oh?"

"I don't hate the hotel."

"Jackson..."

"After all the time we spent together when your family lived there, it was like a second home to me." He slowed his steps. "That's why I didn't consider staying anywhere else when I came back to New Orleans."

"Yes, I suppose we both grew up there."

"I have a lot of good memories in those walls, in spite of how it all ended."

Each time she tried to throw some distance between them, he somehow made it dissolve. *Yes,* she wanted to answer. *We have more good memories than bad. I was your Charlie and you were my best friend...and my first love.*

Charlotte realized with a start that they had reached the entrance to the lot. She could see Desmond, the attendant, dozing on his stool in the kiosk, his head resting against one of the glass walls. The sounds of the Quarter's ongoing party were fainter here, lending an air of hushed intimacy to the darkness.

How many evenings had she and Jackson spent strolling along these darkened streets like this, prolonging their time together? They'd always been loath to say goodbye.

But that was half a lifetime ago, she reminded herself.

"Which one's yours?"

"Mmm? Oh, the beige sedan near the light pole."

He put his palm on the small of her back as they walked through the lot. "As I recall, you used to dream of owning a Corvette like your papa's."

"The sedan's more sensible. It gets excellent gas mileage, too," she added, although she didn't know why she felt it necessary to defend her choice of vehicle.

There were plenty of things she had dreamed about as a teenager that she knew better than to want now.

So it was only a sentimental longing that made her want to step into Jackson's arms and linger over their goodbye. Merely an echo of the past that made her want to feel his fingers in her hair again. Just a side effect of the memories. Nostalgia. Stress. Habit.

She held out her hand. "My car keys are in the briefcase," she said.

He stopped at the rear bumper of her car, dropped the briefcase to the ground and grabbed her arm with his left hand. "Damn, not again!"

"What—"

He pulled her back to his chest and looped his right arm in front of her shoulders. "Hey!" he yelled, turning his head toward the kiosk. "Wake up!"

The attendant didn't stir. Through the corner of her eye Charlotte could see Desmond's motionless form silhouetted against the glass, but she didn't turn her head. She couldn't. Once again she pressed into Jackson's embrace, frozen in shock, and stared at the destruction in front of her.

Every window in her car had been shattered. Crumbs of broken safety glass sparkled from the dashboard and the seats like drifts of blue-tinted sequins. The upholstery had been slashed to ribbons, baring springs and spilling stuffing. A thin, long-bladed knife, like the one that had been driven into her desk the day before, was embedded in the top of the driver's seat headrest.

And trailing from the handle of the knife like some macabre decoration was a string of Mardi Gras beads that had been fashioned into a noose.

CHAPTER FIVE

JACKSON PRESSED HIS head next to hers. His warmth steadied her, enveloping her in his strength. "Deep breaths, Charlie." His lips brushed her ear. "You're okay."

Charlotte breathed hard through her nose, shoving back the urge to scream. Somehow the beads were more frightening than the knife. To shape something harmless, something that should have been fun, into a threat was just…obscene.

"Do you have your phone?" he asked.

"In my pocket."

Still keeping his arm around her shoulders, Jackson patted the front of her suit jacket with his free hand. "I need you to call 911 for me." He slipped the phone from her pocket and held it up. "I'm going to take a look at that attendant, okay?"

She fumbled to take her phone, tearing her gaze away from her car to look at the kiosk. The young man on the stool inside still hadn't stirred. "Go ahead. I—"

"Charlotte? Jackson? Is everything all right?"

At the call, Charlotte looked toward the street. Her mother's car was idling at the entrance to the lot, the interior light on and the driver's door ajar. Anne Marchand was rounding the hood, her expression troubled. As soon as she caught sight of Charlotte's face, she broke into a jog and headed toward her daughter.

Charlotte pulled away from Jackson, concern for her mother overriding everything else. "Mama, I'm fine! Don't run! Please!"

But as usual, Anne ignored Charlotte's caution and covered the distance between them like a woman half her age. "I was just coming home and I saw you both here—" Her gaze went to the car. "Oh, no! What happened?"

"Someone broke my windshield, that's all." She hooked her mother's arm and tried to turn her away from the mess. "I'm calling the police," she said, thumbing 911 into her phone with her free hand.

Jackson paused only long enough to scrutinize Anne's face, then squeezed her shoulder and backed away. "Her color's good, Charlotte," he said, "and she's not out of breath. So don't worry."

Anne whipped her gaze to Jackson. "Jackson Bailey, don't you start treating me like an invalid, too. It's bad enough that my daughter thinks I'm spun sugar."

He didn't take time to reply, turning away from them and loping toward the kiosk. By the time he stepped inside, Charlotte had the emergency operator on the line. While she was giving the location of the parking lot, she watched Jackson try to rouse the attendant.

"What happened to Desmond?" Anne asked.

Charlotte could see the gleam of blood on the attendant's forehead. She told the operator to send an ambulance as well as the police, then put away her phone and took her mother by the shoulders. "There's nothing you can do, Mama," she said. "It might be best if you go home."

"I'm fine, Charlotte. I wish you wouldn't fuss so…" Anne

pressed her hand to her mouth, her eyes widening as she returned her gaze to the car. "Is that a knife?"

"Mama—"

"Mon Dieu!" She shrugged off Charlotte's hold and leaned over to take a closer look at the interior. "And beads? Why in the world would anyone do that?"

Charlotte tried not to moan in frustration. The last thing she wanted to do was cause her mother more worry. She strove for a calm tone. "You know how it is at Mardi Gras. Some people have too much to drink and do foolish things."

"But this is so…gruesome."

"The police will handle it, Mama."

As if on cue, the sound of a siren rose above the traces of music from the other side of the block. Charlotte could see Jackson pressing what looked like a handkerchief to Desmond's forehead with his good hand, evidently doing what he could in spite of his handicap. With relief she noticed that the young man had regained consciousness and was moving on his own.

"It's horrible." Anne crossed her arms and rubbed her hands briskly over her sleeves as if she felt a chill. "I know the city has its problems, but it seems as if our family is seeing far more than our share of crime lately."

Charlotte tried to keep her thoughts from showing on her face, but her mother's comment set off alarms in her head. Detective Fergusson had said something similar the day before. They *had* been experiencing far more problems than was reasonable. This incident of vandalism was obviously deliberate and had targeted her personally, like the last one. But what about the earlier troubles?

It had been all she could do just to get from one day to the next. What if all their troubles hadn't been simply bad luck and coincidence?

She looked at the shadowed street. Just minutes ago the darkness had felt intimate. Now it felt threatening, as if someone was out there watching...

She stooped to pick up the briefcase Jackson had dropped. "I'm going to walk you home, Mama. There's nothing you can do here— Oh!" The briefcase latch must have been damaged when it hit the pavement. The bag sprang open as soon as Charlotte tried to lift it, spilling papers across the ground. She gathered them mechanically, barely looking at them, until a long white envelope caught her eye. She paused to study it and saw that her mother's name was scrawled across the front in black ink.

A knot of ice tightened her stomach. Charlotte knew with complete certainty that she hadn't put this envelope in her briefcase herself.

The last time she'd seen it had been the previous morning, when Dan Corbin had tried to push it into her hands.

MIKE BLOUNT LEANED back into the seat cushions and drummed his fingers against the armrest. Lights from the police car that squeezed past on his left flashed through the tinted windows of the limousine. The vehicle's armor plating muffled most of the noise from the siren, but Mike nevertheless felt an unpleasant rush at the sound.

Richard Corbin craned his neck to watch the cruiser turn down the street toward the parking lot. He sat beside his brother in the seat that faced the back, his leg jerking up and down as his heel thumped rhythmically against the floor.

Trashing the Marchand woman's car had excited him—he hadn't been able to keep still yet.

By contrast, Dan stared out the window, following the police car's progress. "Are you sure you delivered our message, Luc?"

Mike turned his head to look at the man who sat beside him and waited for his reply. Carter had been off balance since he'd seen Mike in the lobby. That had been one of the reasons behind his surprise visit—keeping people off balance made them easier to manage.

"The purchase agreement is in Charlotte's briefcase," Carter replied.

"Excellent," Mike said. "If they don't understand their position by now, they will soon."

Carter tipped his head toward the retreating cruiser. "If the Marchands can put the pieces together, so can the police."

"Don't worry about the police," Mike said. "They won't be a factor."

"You have to keep your cool, Luc," Dan warned him. "The cops still don't have anything to tie us to the Marchands' problems. They can speculate all they want, but there's no direct evidence that would stand up in court."

Richard interrupted his twitching to point at Carter. "You better hope the cops don't come looking, because if they do, you'll be the first one they'll notice."

A muscle jumped in Carter's cheek. "It would help if you quit showing up here. We can't be seen together or the Marchands will stop trusting me."

"Yes," Mike said. "I hear you've made yourself indispensable. That's good. The Marchands wouldn't keep someone around who is no longer of any value to them." He paused deliberately. "Neither would I."

Carter picked at the crease in his right pant leg. "What do we do next?"

Mike looked past Carter to the far side of the street, where the lights of the Hotel Marchand glowed majestically. With the wrought-iron balconies that stretched over the sidewalk and the hanging pots full of greenery it was a classy place, a jewel of the French Quarter. Its reputation was as flawless as its appearance.

And once the hotel was his, he would turn it into a gold mine. Not only was it the perfect location to expand his gambling operation, it would attract the kind of clientele who liked their hookers in a higher income bracket. No more would Mike need to use his syrup company for cover. He would be presiding over one of the most prestigious addresses in the Quarter, rubbing shoulders with the city's elite...and he'd be smiling all the way to his favorite Cayman bank.

"Next?" he repeated. "That depends on how quickly the Marchands accept the Corbins' generous offer."

Richard snickered. "They'll be sorry they waited. The price already went down."

"You need to give them a chance to respond before we stage anything else," Carter said. "They're not going to react well to intimidation."

"Are you telling me how to conduct my business, Luc?" Mike asked, his voice dangerously soft.

"I wouldn't do that."

"Good." Mike flipped open the control panel that was built

into his armrest and pressed a button. The door beside Carter unlocked with a soft click. "You should get back to work before someone notices your absence."

"But—"

"We'll be in touch when we need you again."

Carter reached for the door handle a little too slowly in Mike's opinion. Narrowing his eyes, he watched until the man disappeared into the hotel, then signaled his driver to move off.

The Marchands might be foolish enough to trust Carter, but Mike didn't. He would leave him in place for now, though. The concierge's position on the inside was still of value to him. That idiot Richard had the right idea: if something went wrong with the next phase of the plan, it would be Carter who would take the fall.

CHARLOTTE PULLED THE blanket around her shoulders and picked up her coffee cup, listening to the familiar sounds of the hotel awakening around her. A gray dawn rain pattered against the window of her mother's living room, lending a sense of timelessness to the scene. Although Anne was the only one who currently lived here, Charlotte could feel the presence of the rest of the family.

Sipping her coffee, Charlotte moved her gaze over the framed snapshots that her mother had placed around the room. There was *Grand-mère* Celeste, her chin lifted regally, the impact of her patrician features undiminished in spite of her eighty-four years. On the entry table was a snapshot of Anne with her brother, Pierre, the uncle Charlotte had never met. He'd been a troublemaker in his youth, and the uncompromising Celeste had ordered him out of their home by his eighteenth birthday. Yet Anne still loved him and never had given up hoping she would see him again.

She moved toward the mantel, where she could see her father's bighearted smile. Remy was frozen in time, holding his arms out for baby Melanie to toddle across the lobby carpet. Charlotte looked at the next photo and could almost hear Sylvie's laughter in the courtyard as she chased the bubbles that Renee blew from a plastic wand. And she could still feel the pride in her mother's gaze as she straightened Charlotte's graduation cap. As Jackson had said, there were memories in these walls, as well as so much love.

She tightened her grip on the coffee cup and took an unladylike but fortifying gulp. There was no way she was going to surrender this place, especially not to a pair of vultures like the Corbins. She couldn't. This hotel was her parents' legacy. And it was her life.

But it wasn't only *her* life that was involved, was it?

The suspicions that had taken root in the parking lot yesterday had grown into certainty over the course of the night. She should have seen it before. Yet sensible, responsible Charlotte wasn't given to paranoia any more than she was given to flights of fancy. If there was a rational explanation for something, she would find it. The idea of a deliberate plot against the hotel had seemed too far-fetched to consider.

Yet at what point did rationalization become denial?

The attempted carjacking her mother had fallen victim to was unlikely to have been random. The hit-and-run that Melanie had been involved in the month before couldn't have been an accident. She was sure of that now. And regardless of what

Detective Fergusson claimed, Charlotte suspected faulty wiring hadn't caused this week's fire, either.

Then there were all those problems that had eaten into the hotel's profits. Taken separately, the incidents could be explained away. But once she pulled back to look at the big picture, the pattern that emerged was frightening.

Worse, it was escalating.

Charlotte set her coffee cup on the mantel, braced her fists beside it and regarded the snapshots once more. She'd sheltered her family from the full truth of how grim their finances were, but if she sheltered them from this truth, their ignorance could put them in danger.

Her phone trilled, breaking the hush of the rain-dimmed room. Charlotte pushed away from the mantel and lunged for the chair where she'd left her clothes. She took the phone from her suit jacket before the second ring.

"Hi. Did I wake you?"

Jackson's voice, so steady and familiar, brought his presence into the room as easily as the photographs had brought her family. "No, I'm on my second coffee," she replied.

"How's Anne doing?"

Charlotte glanced down the hall to make sure the door to her mother's bedroom was still closed, then moved over to sit on the sofa where she'd spent the night and tucked the blanket around her shoulders. "Fine. Annoyed with my fussing over her health but happy for my company."

"Did you tell her your suspicions about the Corbins yet?"

Charlotte pressed her free hand to her temple. "You don't beat around the bush, do you?"

"Never have."

"I remember. And, yes, I'm going to tell her. I need to tell my sisters, too. We have to decide how to handle this together."

"Want to hear what I think?"

"That's why you called me, isn't it?"

His low laugh warmed her more than the coffee had. "I called you because I figured phoning would be safer than showing up on your doorstep at this hour. You never were a morning person."

She sighed. "And you were always disgustingly cheerful. You have no idea how many times I was tempted to heave my schoolbooks at your head."

"Why do you think I insisted on carrying them for you?"

"How did you get my cell number anyway?"

"Melanie gave it to me when I went down to the kitchen."

"What were you doing there?"

"Stealing pastry." He sounded as if he were chewing. "It's not as good as your papa's was, but it's close. Want some?"

No matter how much she tried to remind herself that the past was over, it was far too tempting to slip into the old, comfortable pattern. She and Jackson had spent hours on the phone like this. They used to be able to talk about nothing as easily as they had shared their innermost thoughts.

She slid down on the sofa until her head rested against the arm. "Weren't you about to let me know what you think?"

"Right." His voice sobered. "I realize you're concerned about Anne's heart condition. You'd probably feel better if I were there to keep an eye on her when you tell her about the Corbins' threats."

"Jackson…"

"Before you say the hotel isn't my business, remember I

was with you when we found the Corbins' handiwork in your office and your car. We spoke to the police together, so I'm already involved."

"Yes, but—"

"Charlotte, let me help you."

It might have been due to fatigue or because she could hear echoes of the boy who'd been her best friend in the voice of this man. Whatever the reason, Jackson's softly spoken offer stole through her defenses.

Pride made her want to refuse, but she forced herself to think logically. Jackson was already involved. And having someone with medical training nearby during the upcoming meeting would indeed ease her worry about causing her mother more stress. In order to keep the hotel, Charlotte could use all the help she could get. "I can't lose this place, Jackson."

"I understand."

From someone else the phrase would have been a meaningless platitude, but not from Jackson. Charlotte knew that he understood what she was going through on a level that no one else could. "We can't lock the shutters and barricade ourselves in here, either, or the hotel would go out of business for sure. We need to make this Mardi Gras a success."

"Yes, you do."

"And I'm certainly not going to run scared from a pair of thugs, no matter what they try."

"I know you wouldn't."

"But I don't have the right to ask my family to take the same risk."

"If your family is anything like the way I remember," Jackson said, "you won't need to ask."

"THIS IS OUTRAGEOUS!" Anne Marchand stabbed a polished fingernail in the center of the document, crumpling the paper against the table from the force of her gesture. Twin spots of angry color darkened her cheeks. "These men are no better than thieves."

All four of the Marchand sisters reacted at once. As Sylvie hummed soothing noises and Melanie offered Anne a glass of ice water, Renee gently patted her mother's hand, allowing Charlotte to whisk the purchase offer from the table and return it to her briefcase.

Anne regarded each of her daughters in turn, giving them a quelling look that only a mother could manage. Love and exasperation mixed in equal parts.

Jackson pulled one of the extra dining chairs away from the wall, reversed it and straddled the seat. As he'd hoped, Anne was holding up well and showed no signs of needing a doctor's services. Even at sixty-two she was as vibrant a woman as ever. Folding his arms across the chair back, he settled in to watch the byplay between Anne and her strong-willed daughters.

He'd always admired Anne Marchand. In spite of the fact her mother, Celeste, hadn't deigned to remain in the same room with him, Anne had been unfalteringly kind. She had never made any reference to his mother's background or his father's lack of wealth. Anne had treated him fairly when he'd been a kid, giving him the run of a place that his own parents couldn't have afforded to enter.

The exclusive private dining room that Charlotte was using for the meeting was tucked into the back of the hotel restaurant. It had the same elegant linen-and-old-wood ambience of the main room on a smaller and more personal scale. Although Charlotte's mother and sisters had been surprised to see that she had included Jackson in their family conference, they'd accepted his presence once they'd learned what had transpired during the past two days. Charlotte's sisters hadn't come to this meeting alone either—they'd brought their fiancés.

While the discussion at the table turned to the subject of how to deal with the Corbins, Jackson glanced at the other men in the room. He'd met Robert LeSoeur, Melanie's fiancé, in the kitchen earlier. But Jefferson Lambert, Sylvie's fiancé, had been a surprise. The buttoned-down New England lawyer looked like the last person a free spirit like Sylvie would have chosen. The third man, Renee's beau, hadn't needed an introduction: Pete Traynor was a Hollywood director with leading-man looks that the tabloids loved. Jackson had recognized him on sight.

As different from one another as these three men were, their expressions of concern were almost identical.

"Why can't the cops arrest them?" Pete demanded. "It's obvious the Corbins have crossed the line."

Charlotte looked past Renee to where Pete stood beside the window. "Jackson and I spoke with Detective Fergusson about the Corbins on Wednesday and again yesterday. Fergusson said he questioned them already, but he has no grounds to arrest them because there's no evidence they've done anything illegal. Until he gets some proof, he can't touch them."

"That's the problem with police," Jefferson commented, his rich courtroom voice filling the small room. "By definition, they have to uphold the law, while the suspects they pursue aren't hampered by it."

"Fergusson is hiding behind that excuse," Jackson said.

"He didn't strike me as someone who would go out of his way to solve a case."

"Didn't you like him?" Robert asked.

"No. He seems too good-humored for a cop. I got the feeling he was only going through the motions."

"At least now we know what we're up against," Renee said. "That knowledge gives us an advantage."

"So does the timetable the Corbins specified," Charlotte added. "Their offer expires after Mardi Gras."

Jackson glanced at the briefcase where she had put the Corbins' offer. "It's interesting that they would choose Mardi Gras as their deadline. If their goal is to obtain the hotel, why set a time limit that's only a few days away?"

"They obviously realize that if we have a successful season, they won't have a chance of acquiring the hotel," Charlotte replied.

"Then this should be over next week."

Charlotte dipped her chin. "Yes, it should be. One way or another. Mac and I plan to keep the hotel security on high alert throughout the next several days to minimize any possible risk to our guests, but it appears the Corbins have shifted their focus. The recent vandalism has targeted my personal property rather than the hotel's."

"A strategic move," Jefferson said. "They've decided it's more effective to harass the people who control the hotel rather than the hotel itself."

"But those knives…" Sylvie shuddered, setting the bracelets she wore at her wrists jangling. "Charlotte, it makes my flesh crawl. If the Corbins were bold enough to strike at your office and your car, what's next? A horse head in your bed?

No offense to Renee and Pete, but this is like something out of a bad Mob movie."

"It's all too real," Charlotte said. "I underestimated the lengths the Corbins would go to, so I was slow to grasp the connection between them and our recent problems. I apologize for that and take full responsibility. While I plan to continue with my duties, I don't expect the rest of you to—"

"Charlotte Anne Marchand," Anne said sharply. "This has gone far enough. When will you realize you don't have to carry us on your shoulders?"

"Mama—"

"That's right," Melanie chimed in. "You're still doing the big-sister thing. This is our problem, too."

"Well put," Renee said. "The Corbins are the ones who made the mistake, not you, Charlotte. They chose the wrong target for their scare tactics."

Sylvie leaned across the table and grasped Charlotte's hand. "You're not alone, *chérie*."

"We won't give in to those cowards." Melanie clasped her sisters' joined hands.

An instant later, so did Renee. "There's strength in numbers. With all four of us—"

"Five," Anne corrected, placing her hand over those of her daughters. "Don't any of you forget I am still the official owner of this hotel. Under no circumstances will I see what your papa and I built go to a pair of *cochons* who masquerade as businessmen."

Charlotte's eyes were luminous as she gazed around the table. "Before you promise anything, I have to tell you that

Detective Fergusson has already stated the police can't give us any protection."

"I wouldn't want to rely on Fergusson anyway," Pete said, striding forward. He stopped behind Renee's chair and squeezed her shoulders. "As you said, Renee, there's strength in numbers. Until the Corbins' Mardi Gras deadline is safely passed, I don't plan to let you out of my sight."

Jefferson cleared his throat. "While I second Pete's macho sentiment and will be keeping a close watch over my darling Sylvie and Daisy Rose, we need more than that. None of us is trained in security."

"Mac is," Robert said. "He can advise us on other measures to take that might reduce our risk."

"This sounds good," Anne said. "I know William would insist on protecting me if he could be here, but since he isn't, I'll move in with *Grand-mère*. Charlotte, you should, too. Her house is well fortified against intruders. We can assign someone from hotel security to escort you during the day."

"My home is perfectly safe," Charlotte said, withdrawing her hand from the other women's. "The security staff need to concentrate on the safety of the hotel and our guests, and I wouldn't want to put an extra strain on their resources simply because I'm an unattached female. I believe the Corbins want to scare us, not physically harm us, so as long as I'm cautious and remain on my guard—"

"You're doing it again," Melanie said, pointing at her sister. "Worrying about everyone else instead of yourself."

Jackson saw Charlotte lift her chin as she always did when she was about to argue. He spoke before she could. "I'll stay with you, Charlotte."

The silence that followed his remark was eloquent. While her sisters exchanged interested glances, Charlotte retrieved her briefcase and rose to her feet. "Thanks, Jackson," she said. "I realize you want to help, but it wouldn't be fair to impose on you this way."

"It wouldn't be an imposition. It's a sensible solution." He grasped the back of his chair and swung it aside as he stood. "I know how bullies like the Corbins operate. I've seen the same principle in every corrupt regime and dictatorship around the world. The scope might vary, but the methods don't. They only pick easy targets, so your family is right— you can't appear to be alone."

"My house is small."

"That wouldn't bother me. I've slept in a mud hut."

She held her briefcase to her chest. "You'd have to keep up with me while I work."

"I know the layout of the hotel as well as anyone else who works here. It would be easy for me to watch out for you."

"He has a point, *chérie*," Anne said. She flicked her gaze between Charlotte and Jackson, then folded her hands together and regarded him carefully. "And judging from what I've seen since you've come home, Jackson, you've already been watching out for Charlotte."

Her words made him pause. His offer was meant to be practical, but Anne had made it sound…personal.

Renee arched one eyebrow and looked at her sisters. Melanie grinned as Sylvie winked.

Jackson swallowed a groan. Those looks were familiar. He and Charlotte used to get the same reactions twenty years ago when they'd been caught necking under the stairs.

CHAPTER SIX

CHARLOTTE HAD NEVER considered her home small before. It wasn't large—it could fit into one corner of her grandmother's mansion—yet the quaint Creole cottage suited her needs. It had been a good investment, since the neighborhood bordered on the French Quarter and had gradually become more gentrified. It was inviting at first sight, with its gingerbread trim and the graceful live oak that arched over the front yard. Charlotte had decorated the rooms the same way she'd seen her mother acquire furnishings for the hotel, scouring antique stores and estate sales to find pieces that evoked the region's rich history. She'd gone for quality rather than quantity, keeping the lines clean and the colors light, so the house didn't appear crowded by any means.

That is, until Jackson Bailey had stepped inside.

His presence filled the space around him instantly. He should have looked out of place against the backdrop of polished wood, cream-colored upholstery and delicate rose-patterned wallpaper. Instead he appeared completely at home, as if all the femininity around him had been waiting for a man to balance it.

"It's you, Charlotte," he said, following her into the living room.

"Mmm?"

"This house." He dropped his pack beside the sofa. "Your personality is all over it."

"Thank you." She switched on the lamp beside the book-case, hoping some extra illumination would dispel the cozy atmosphere. Instead the soft yellow light emphasized the chiseled hollows and angles of Jackson's face, making Char-lotte more conscious than ever of how masculine he looked.

She grasped for a neutral topic. "Fortunately this neighbor-hood is on relatively high ground, so we escaped much of the flood damage that other areas have had to deal with."

"How long have you lived here?"

She moved to the front window and closed the drapes. "Almost twelve years."

"That explains it."

"Explains what?"

"It doesn't look like the kind of place Adrian would have liked," he said.

She'd told him the topic of her marriage was off-limits, but he wasn't talking about that, he was talking about the house. And his insight was completely correct. Adrian would have consid-ered residing in this small yet picturesque bungalow beneath his dignity. He'd insisted on living in an echoing old mausoleum of a house that had been a block from her grandmother's place.

She watched Jackson tilt his head as he studied the water-color landscape that hung above the pecan side table. The lock of hair that never seemed to stay in place flopped over his fore-head. He was wearing faded jeans and a V-neck navy-blue sweater today. It wasn't a thick sweater. The wool was fine enough to mold every curve and ridge of his wide shoulders.

Adrian had been fastidious about his appearance, seldom appearing in public without a suit and tie, even in the summer. He'd been blessed with exceptionally handsome features, a dazzling smile and soulful brown eyes. He'd been the quintessential Southern gentleman. Everyone had agreed that she and her husband had made a lovely couple.

But Adrian at his best couldn't compare to Jackson with mussed hair and old jeans.

Charlotte rubbed her temples. How could she notice Jackson's looks at a time like this? Did she want to play right into her sisters' hands? Those women were acting as if she were back in high school—their winks and nudges had been following her from the moment the family conference had adjourned.

She had good reasons—logical reasons—for having Jackson stay with her. It had nothing to do with the fact that she used to be in love with him. He was just an old friend who was helping her out. The crisis at the hotel was Charlotte's top priority. Rekindling a romance was the last thing on her mind.

"Is something wrong?" Jackson asked. "Do you have a headache?"

She shook her head and adjusted a fold of the drapes, then moved back to the bookcase and straightened one of the photos of Daisy Rose that rested on top. "I was just thinking about my family," she said. "They mean well, but I hope you understand that you're free to change your mind about staying here."

"Why would I change my mind?"

"I realize you have problems of your own to deal with," she said. "It's very generous of you to want to help me with mine, but—"

"If by problems you mean this," he said, holding up his

right hand, "there's nothing much I can do until Yves finishes his tests and gives me his prognosis. You're doing me a favor, not the other way around."

"How's that?"

"Waiting is hell. I'd rather keep busy."

She should have thought of that. Of course Jackson would want to take his mind off his own situation. *That's* why he'd been so quick to appoint himself her bodyguard. It was in his nature to help wherever he saw a need, but he also needed a distraction.

In light of that, worrying about how this arrangement might look seemed petty. She and Jackson were both facing far bigger concerns. Her reservations dissolved. "Thanks, Jackson," she said. "I do appreciate your help, and if there's anything I can do to return the favor, please let me know."

He lowered his hand to his side. "If you were offering me an out because you think I won't be capable of being any use to you with my disability—"

"Oh, no," she said hurriedly. "That's not the issue. It never entered my mind."

"It's only my right hand that doesn't work. Everything else still does. If any trouble comes up, I'll be calling the police anyway."

She waved her hands in front of her as if clearing away what he had said. "I told you, Jackson, that's not the issue. I just don't want people to get the wrong idea."

"Ah," he said, the corner of his mouth lifting into one of his lopsided smiles. "I get it now. This is about those looks your sisters gave us."

"You noticed?"

"It was hard to miss. They were about as subtle as three-month-old shrimp."

"And that doesn't bother you?"

"Actually they were kind of cute. It reminded me of the old days."

"How? Because they were pains then, too?"

"Sometimes. They used to be inordinately fascinated by our relationship then, as well."

"I'll make it clear to them that we're just friends."

"Sure, if that's what you want to call it."

There was no chance to respond, even if she'd known what to say. In the next instant her phone began to ring. She slipped it from her jacket pocket and pressed it to her ear.

"Hello, Miss Marchand."

At the raspy male voice, she froze. "Who is this?" she demanded.

In a few swift strides Jackson moved around the sofa to where she stood. Pressing close to her side, he clasped her wrist and tipped the phone away from her ear so that he could listen with her.

A phlegmy cough sounded through the receiver. "Archie Manning," the caller said, his voice smoothing into one she recognized. "From Manning Insurance."

She blew out a relieved breath. It was only their insurance agent, not Richard Corbin, as she'd thought when she'd first heard him. "Oh, hello, Mr. Manning. How are you?"

"As you can hear, the cold I seem to have picked up is doing fine, but I'm not so sure about myself."

"I'm sorry to hear that."

"I called to give you an update on your claim."

Charlotte glanced sideways at Jackson. He was still holding her wrist, his head inches from hers. She tugged lightly, trying to free her hand, but he didn't let go. "Which claim do you mean, Mr. Manning?" she asked. "The car or the hotel?"

He coughed again. "I haven't had a chance to process the claim for your car yet and, unfortunately, I have some bad news for you on the other. I've just seen the official report on the fire. It was caused by faulty wiring."

"Detective Fergusson told me the investigation isn't complete."

"It appears to be now. I'm sorry, Miss Marchand. According to the terms of the policy, we can't allow the claim if your own negligence caused the damage."

She frowned. This didn't make sense. She'd been sure the Corbins had set that fire. "I'm familiar with the terms of our policy. This couldn't have been negligence. We used licensed contractors with every renovation. We took all reasonable precautions."

"I'm sorry," he repeated. "The report was very clear. There's nothing I can do."

She strove to maintain her calm in spite of the dread that was gnawing at her stomach. Cleaning up after that fire had wiped out the last of their reserve fund. She'd been counting on the insurance settlement. "The total of the premiums we have paid over the past several years far exceeds the amount of this claim, Mr. Manning. Surely there is some room to negotiate—"

"You'll have to take that up with your contractor. Goodbye, Miss Marchand."

The connection terminated. Jackson loosened his grip on

her wrist and tipped his head away from hers. "That's strange," he said.

She lowered the phone. "It's more than strange, it's a disaster. We can't afford this."

"I meant the police report. Why would Fergusson move so fast on that when he doesn't seem to put much effort into anything else?"

Not for the first time Charlotte wished that the case had gone to someone more competent, like Detective Rothberg, instead of Fergusson. "I'm afraid I share your doubts over his abilities."

"He was either too lazy to do a thorough job or he was deliberately cutting it short."

"I'm going to get an explanation," she said, dialing Fergusson's number. Instead of the detective, she got a recorded message. Frustrated, she hit the disconnect with enough force to bend her fingernail double.

"What?" Jackson asked.

"He's gone for the day. An insurance agent with a cold is still at work, but our police detective isn't." She jabbed another number. "I'm going to call Manning back. How dare he try to slide out of his obligations."

Jackson plucked the phone from her grasp. "Maybe you'd better take a few deep breaths instead."

She held out her palm. "Give me the phone."

"I'd better not," he said, placing the phone on the bookcase beside the photos. "You look as if you're going to throw it."

"Jackson—"

"Take some deep breaths."

"Oh, for heaven's sake," she muttered, reaching past him.

He caught her hand and lifted it between them. "Your fist is clenched and your pulse is racing. This isn't good for you, Charlotte."

"You might have appointed yourself my bodyguard, but you're not my therapist."

"I don't want to see you stress yourself into a heart attack twenty years from now the way Anne did."

"You're not my doctor either."

"Don't be stubborn. I'm only trying to help."

"I don't want your pity, Jackson."

He brought their joined hands to his chest. "Then what do you want?"

Oh, that was the wrong question, especially when he was holding her hand. The awareness of how close they stood had been simmering in some part of her mind since she'd answered the phone. She'd done her best to ignore it, but she couldn't any longer. She drew her lower lip between her teeth, wondering whether he realized there were reasons other than stress for her racing pulse.

He turned his wrist, twining her forearm with his to pull her closer. "Okay, since you're not talking, how about if I tell you what I want?"

She looked at his mouth. He wasn't smiling, but that didn't seem to matter. She could feel his smile in the slide of his arm against hers and the easy grasp of his fingers. "What?"

"Better yet, I'll show you."

"Jackson…"

He pulled her clear from the bookcase and wrapped his arms behind her back.

He'd held her before, twice, but this time it was different.

There was no tension in his frame or anxiety in his touch. His warmth surrounded her like an invitation, coaxing her to relax and join him.

Charlotte managed to hold out for a full ten seconds. She counted them off, keeping her fists clenched and her back stiff as her mind went through the familiar litany. She had too much to do. Too many people depended on her. She had to stay in control. She should be thinking of the hotel, not of herself.

But this felt so good, how could she fight it? What harm would there be if she stayed where she was for a little while longer? Sighing, she closed her eyes and dropped her forehead against Jackson's shoulder.

And as easily as that a rush of familiar sensations tingled through her body. Her senses remembered the feel of him. It was like seeing a photograph from her childhood or catching the aroma of her grandmother's magnolias. A forgotten pleasure was within her grasp once more. The need to return the embrace sliced through her reason, and her hands slid around his waist to lock behind his back.

He widened his stance so that she could step closer. The outsides of her shoes brushed the insides of his boots and more sense memories crashed over her. They were fitting together the same way they used to. The bones in his shoulder weren't as sharp as before—a layer of muscle padded the hollow— but she still found the spot where she'd loved to nestle. The fresh scent of night air clung to his sweater, just as it had when he used to walk her home.

He pressed his cheek to the top of her head. "I've wanted to do this for three days."

"It's not a good idea."

"Hell, I know that. Why do you think I waited three days?"

She couldn't believe the laugh that rose to her lips. How could she feel like laughing when she was doing something so stupid?

But this was how it used to be, too. There had never been anything logical about their relationship. They'd been honest about that, too.

His breath blew gently across her hair. "Do you want me to let you go?"

"Not yet."

He moved his hand to the back of her neck and sifted the ends of her hair through his fingers. "Imagine that," he murmured. "It's different, but it still feels the same."

She knew he was referring to her straightened hair, but he could have been talking about everything else. The past was mixing with the present, giving an extra dimension to what she felt now. And for an instant, she almost was his Charlie again...

The thought alarmed her. What on earth was she doing? As tempting as it was, she couldn't afford to let the old feelings stir. Nothing could come of this—it was only stress mixed with nostalgia. It would be madness to confuse it with anything more.

She opened her eyes and blinked them into focus, only to discover her nose was on a level with the base of Jackson's throat. The scent of hotel soap and male skin overwhelmed the memories. So did the glimpse of crisp dark hair and the muscular contours that she could see down the loose neckline of his sweater. The last time she'd seen Jackson's bare chest, he'd had only a few fine hairs in the center.

Her gaze moved up to his jaw, lingering on the hint of beard shadow along the edge. When she'd known him, he'd only needed to shave every other day. That had obviously changed, too. She tipped back her head to look at his face.

The shift in her balance brought her lower body more firmly against his, and the heat that shot through her from the contact had nothing to do with nostalgia. Behind the barrier of his denim jeans she could feel the long, hard length of his erection.

There was no way to confuse the fact that she was being held by a man, not a boy.

Jackson met her gaze squarely. His pupils had expanded, making the blue that remained more intense than she'd ever seen it. He had to realize that she was aware of the reaction of his body, yet he made no attempt to conceal it. Instead he closed his fingers over a lock of her hair and boldly dropped his gaze to her mouth.

There were no nerve endings in her hair, yet she could still feel his caress. Only his gaze touched her mouth, but her lips tingled as if he were stroking her. Her breasts swelled against his chest and her pulse throbbed, warm and heavy.

She couldn't confuse this with a memory, either. It was too vivid, too…new. She hadn't felt such a strong physical reaction to Jackson in the past, yet she'd lost count of the number of times he had stirred this response in the last three days.

The sexual awareness had to be a side effect of the circumstances, she reasoned. It was completely natural, nothing to be distressed about. It would only become a problem if they let things go further.

She spread her fingers quickly, unlocking her grip from Jackson's waist.

"Charlotte…"

She held up her palm to stop whatever he was going to say. She hoped he wouldn't notice that her hand was shaking. "I need to check in with the hotel," she said, stepping back. "I'll use the phone in the kitchen."

GRITTING HIS TEETH, Jackson slid into the steaming water until his head rested on the rim of the bathtub. There was no shower in Charlotte's bathroom, only a vintage claw-footed tub that wasn't designed for a man his size. He had to fold his knees in half and angle his elbows over the sides just to fit himself in, but it was good for one thing—already he could feel the heat loosening his tensed muscles.

The night on Charlotte's sofa had left his body in knots. That particular piece of furniture hadn't been designed for a large man either, yet he knew that wasn't the main reason for his discomfort. It was from staying awake half the night thinking about how he'd rather have been in Charlotte's bed.

It was his own fault. He shouldn't have touched her. And once he had, he should have maintained better control over his thoughts. Yes, Charlotte was a desirable woman, but he wasn't some randy teenager anymore, he was a mature, responsible man.

The problem was, he was also mature enough to recognize when desire was mutual. There had been no mistaking the way Charlotte's body had softened against his when she'd nestled into his arms. He'd seen her eyes darken and felt the surprised puff of her breath as her lips had parted. That hadn't been the first time it had happened, either, and the knowledge only added to his restlessness.

It was a good thing she'd had the sense to walk away, right?

He thudded his head back against the tub. He couldn't let himself get drawn into anything with her again. It was worse than pointless. Their bodies and the ages on their driver's licences might have changed, but nothing else had. The hotel was still Charlotte's priority, just as it had been twenty years ago. Once this threat to her business was over, she wouldn't need him anymore. And that was good, because if Yves could repair his hand—

No, not if. When. He still wouldn't allow himself to consider the alternative.

He lifted his right wrist from the water, scowled at his lax fingers, then twisted his head to look at the watch he'd left on top of his clothes. He wanted to stop by the hospital to visit Uncle William again before he took Charlotte to the hotel this morning, and if he was going to manage shaving left-handed without slitting his throat, he couldn't afford to rush. He unfolded himself from the tub and grabbed a towel.

Charlotte was already up by the time he reached the kitchen. Even though it was a Saturday, she was dressed in an ivory silk blouse and a tailored jade skirt. A matching jade suit jacket was draped over the back of a wicker chair. She stood at the window that overlooked a small terrace, early-morning sunlight gilding her delicate features and streaking her hair with gold. The quality of the light and the elegance of her appearance made her look as if she could have stepped straight out of an Impressionist painting…if she hadn't been holding a coffee cup in one hand and a telephone receiver in the other.

"It would be wonderful if you could contact the people on that list," she said. "Thanks, Renee. Oh, Genevieve left a message. She said our costumes are ready." She paused. "Okay, I'll see you later."

Jackson waited in the doorway while she terminated the call. "I didn't expect you to be awake already," he said.

She put the phone on a small glass-topped wicker table that rested beneath the window. A fax machine sat near one edge, a sheaf of papers stacked in front of it. "I had a lot to do. Would you like some coffee?" She nodded toward the coffee-maker on the sideboard. "I usually have breakfast at the hotel, so I'm afraid I don't have much else to offer you."

"I take it you still don't cook?"

"Not if I can avoid it." She glanced at his chest, then quickly averted her gaze. "I leave that to the people who are good at it."

He realized he hadn't yet fastened his shirt buttons. He pulled the sides together and began with the bottom one. "It sounded as if you've already started working."

"Yes. I've been thinking things over and I have to admit I share your lack of confidence in Detective Fergusson. I decided it would be best to get some other opinions about the cause of the fire."

He fumbled the first button into the hole and started on the next. "How?"

"First I'm having Mac and Tyrell get detailed statements from the staff who were there that night. In addition, Renee's going to contact all the emergency personnel who responded to the fire. She knows how to get in touch with them, since she had invited everyone to breakfast at the hotel." She took a long sip from her mug. "We thought if we found enough people who don't agree with Fergusson's finding, we could force the police to reopen the investigation into the fire. At the very least, we should get some ammunition to make a stronger case with the insurance company."

"Sounds good. I'll add my input."

"Thanks."

"If you're lucky, you might uncover something that can lead the police back to the Corbins."

"That would be the best-case scenario, all right." She hesitated, glancing back at his chest. "Do you want some help with those?"

He shoved the next button closed. "No, it's okay. It takes me a while, but I'll get there."

She chewed her lip briefly, then took another mug from a glass-fronted cabinet and filled it with coffee. Without asking, she added two spoons of sugar and a few drops of cream, just the way he used to take it. He liked the fact that she had remembered, so he didn't tell her he preferred to take it black now.

"Is that the reason you're wearing cowboy boots?" she asked. "Because they don't have laces?"

He cocked his head to glance at the scuffed leather toes of his boots. "No, that's a habit I picked up years ago. I found they were faster to get on than sneakers. They lasted longer, too, which was an advantage when there weren't any stores around."

She carried the mugs to the table and sat in the chair where she'd draped her jacket. "Your life has been so different from mine, it's difficult for me to imagine."

He buttoned his right cuff but had to leave the left one undone. He took the chair opposite hers. "I live part of each year in Philadelphia, too. Operating on paying customers is how I pay my own bills."

"But you prefer to be overseas, don't you?"

"That's where I can do the most good."

"What's it like, Jackson? Traveling the world, working in disaster zones and refugee camps?"

"It's hard to generalize because each place has its own unique flavor, just like New Orleans."

"Then tell me something specific."

The first scenes that rose to his mind were too grim to bring into this sunlit room. He searched for one that he could share. "I spent a few weeks in Kashmir after the earthquake in '05. The mountains were beautiful, in a raw, powerful way that stole my breath every morning." He slid the sweetened coffee toward him, still sifting through the memories. "I was thankful for my boots then. The rains that came right after the quake soaked everything. The town's hospital wasn't safe to work in, so we set up shop in makeshift tents, only they leaked like sieves."

"How did you cope?"

"One day the parents of a patient I was working on rigged up a canopy from a piece of plastic and some metal rods from a wrecked bus. They stood on each side of me and made sure the operating table was dry while I set their son's leg. After that, they passed their improvised umbrella to the next family." He smiled. "Problem was, the next bunch was only kids, none of them tall enough to keep that contraption above my head, so they took turns sitting on each other's shoulders to hold it up. I had a hell of a time keeping the stitches straight because they kept knocking into me."

"Who were you stitching?"

"Their mother. That's why I couldn't order them out of the

tent. She'd been seriously injured while she'd been digging her kids out from the rubble of their house. She got frantic if one of them stepped out of her sight."

Charlotte's eyes misted. She reached out to fasten the button on his left cuff. "I've never known a man who is as compassionate as you are, Jackson. They're lucky you were there."

"The work never stops."

"No, it doesn't."

He looked at his right hand where it rested on the glass tabletop in front of him. Frustration with his handicap was never far from the surface, but he wouldn't allow himself to start complaining. Compared to others he'd seen, he really was one of the lucky ones.

"You might not realize this," Charlotte murmured, "but I always admired you for sticking to your ideals, even when I resented you for leaving."

"Same goes for me. You always knew exactly where you belonged."

She nodded. "We both did."

"It's ironic that we find ourselves back together now, isn't it?"

"I had the same thought myself."

Silence fell between them. It wasn't awkward, yet it wasn't comfortable either. The old argument was still there, unresolved and waiting. Something more needed to be said. "Charlotte, I've never had any illusions that I'm saving the world, but if I can save one more person, I have to keep doing it."

"I know you do." She brushed her fingertips over the red line on the back of his hand. "And I understand that you'll go back as soon as you're able to. That's who you are."

Her touch was featherlight, and the area where her fingers

rested had recovered less than sixty percent of normal sensation, yet at her caress, his body responded as quickly as it had the night before. Without thinking, he turned his hand over to clasp hers.

His fingers didn't have the strength to hold her in place, yet she didn't pull away. Even when he rose from his chair, braced his other hand on the table and leaned across the space between them, she didn't retreat. He focused on her lips. "It wouldn't be a good idea if I kissed you right now, would it?"

"No, it wouldn't."

"Worse than holding you yesterday?"

"Much worse."

He leaned closer. "Then I'll make it quick, okay?"

"Jackson, we both know this can't go anywhere—"

He touched his lips to hers, ending her protest. She sighed through her nose, her breath warming his cheek, and tipped her face closer to his. She tasted of toothpaste, coffee and the girl who used to giggle when he would tug her into a corner to steal a kiss.

It had all been so simple then. Easy and innocent. The attraction they'd felt for each other had been a source of joy, and they'd never thought to suppress it. They hadn't known any better.

They did now. He felt Charlotte's restraint in the faint tremor of her lips. Neither of them had closed their eyes—he could see the caution in her green gaze as clearly as he could see her interest.

Damn, he wanted to linger. He wanted to explore the woman she was now. But off balance as he was and leaning over a glass-topped table that held two steaming mugs and a fax machine, he couldn't make the kiss any more than a light brush of their mouths.

It was just as well. He already had enough problems with a wound that wouldn't heal.

He didn't want to reopen one that was twenty years old.

CHAPTER SEVEN

"IT'S LOVELY!" Renee exclaimed. She grasped a fold of Charlotte's skirt to hold it out to the side. "Genevieve has outdone herself this time. You're going to be the belle of our Mardi Gras ball."

Charlotte turned back and forth in front of the dressing room mirror, trying to regard the gown objectively, yet that was as pointless as trying to analyze a beautiful sunset. This was something that had to be felt.

Genevieve Gagnon was as much an artist as she was a seamstress. She'd been designing and making Mardi Gras costumes for the Marchands for as long as Charlotte could remember. Her workmanship was exquisite, and this dress was no exception.

Loops of white sequins glittered from satin the color of the sky on a dusky summer evening. Drifts of delicate white feathers trimmed the edges of the diaphanous sleeves and the hem of the skirt that flowed to the floor. The effect was as whimsical as the matching mask had been, evoking the impression of a fairy-tale princess.

"It's a work of art, Genevieve," Charlotte said. "I don't know how you manage to top yourself every year."

Genevieve chuckled and stabbed her finger at her wheelchair controls to propel herself toward the long, low table in the corner. The tiny white-haired woman was a dynamo, her spirit undiminished in spite of the waterskiing accident that had cost her the use of her legs several years ago. She brushed a heap of colorful fabric scraps from the table and picked up a small book. "I confess I cheated this year, Miss Charlotte."

"How could you possibly cheat?"

She held out the book. "This was my inspiration."

Charlotte gasped in surprised recognition as she took the book from Genevieve. "This looks like the book of fairy tales Papa gave me when I was a kid."

"It is," Renee said.

"How…"

"Miss Renee lent it to me," Genevieve said, her face crinkling into a grin. "She thought you would enjoy seeing it come to life."

Renee nodded. "I got the idea when you started to read some of the stories to Daisy Rose. She seems to enjoy them as much as you did."

"The book's still a bit old for her, but she loved the pictures," Charlotte said. "Especially the depiction of Sleeping Beauty…" She paused to glance at herself in the mirror, then flipped through the book to the illustration at the end of the story.

For a moment, all she could do was stare. She knew the picture well. It had fired her imagination as a child, setting an impossibly romantic ideal. Against the misty backdrop of an ivy-cloaked castle, in front of an audience of smiling forest creatures, Sleeping Beauty had awakened and was waltzing with her handsome prince. The elegant dusky blue gown she wore winked with jewels and swept daintily behind her to blend with the feathery edge of a cloud.

"I can't believe this," Charlotte said. "You did bring it to life, Genevieve. I should have recognized it right away."

"It's perfect," Renee said. "You look exactly like the picture." She smiled. "Now all we need to complete the scene is Prince Charming."

A pang of longing took Charlotte unawares. She closed the book and put it back on the table, then reached under her arm to unfasten the zipper that was concealed in the side seam. She was careful to keep her movements steady, but she felt as if she couldn't get the dress off fast enough. What she really wanted to do was rip it from her body and somehow shove it back into that book of fairy tales.

Because that's where dreams of Prince Charming and happily ever after belonged.

But she had to be practical. This was a costume, nothing more. The Mardi Gras ball was about business, not make-believe. Her guests would expect her to get into the spirit of the occasion. So would her family. She was simply being oversensitive

"Thank you, Genevieve," Charlotte said, pulling up the dress so she could ease her arms out of the sleeves. "Renee is right, you've outdone yourself this time."

"It's my pleasure, Miss Charlotte." Genevieve cocked her head as a bell tinkled from the other side of the curtain that separated the dressing room from her shop. She steered her chair toward the doorway. "I'll be right outside. Let me know if you need anything else."

The curtain swung back into place as a low murmur of male voices drifted through it.

"It sounds as if Pete and Jackson got impatient waiting for

us," Renee said, moving behind Charlotte to help her slip the dress over her head.

"I'm sure Genevieve will keep them entertained."

Renee put the dress on a hanger and carried it to a wheeled wardrobe rack that was jammed with a rainbow array of other Mardi Gras costumes. "She'll flirt with them shamelessly, you know," she said. "Are you sure you want Jackson out there?"

Charlotte grabbed her skirt and yanked it on. "He can do what he likes. It makes no difference to me."

"You've put it on inside out."

"What?"

"Your skirt."

"Yes, I can see that," Charlotte muttered, taking it off. She fixed it impatiently, then pulled on her blouse. "Thanks so much for your help."

"You seem distracted."

Charlotte looked around for her shoes. "No, I just have a lot to do today. Did you get any responses yet from the emergency personnel?"

"Some. Nothing promising so far, but it's only been a few hours. I'm trying to contact Detective Rothberg. He seemed more capable than Fergusson."

"I agree. He appeared more capable, but I was told he wasn't available."

"Well, I'm not giving up."

"None of us will."

"And while we're on the subject of not giving up, how are things going with you and Jackson?"

Charlotte slipped her feet into her heels and walked over to Renee. "I know you mean well," she said, pitching her voice low so it wouldn't carry to the next room. "But I don't want to talk about Jackson. We're just friends."

"That sounds familiar. It's what I tried to tell everyone about Pete and me."

"This situation is different. With the current crisis at the hotel, I don't have the time to think about getting involved with anyone."

"The excuse doesn't wash, Charlotte. A crisis is exactly the time you need someone beside you."

"That's not why Jackson and I are staying together."

"Isn't it?"

Charlotte pressed her fingertips to her temples and rubbed at the tension that was forming there. She realized she was doing that particular gesture far too often lately. "Simply because Jackson and I are living under the same roof doesn't mean anything will happen. It can't. Neither of us wants it to."

Renee walked to the chair where they'd left their purses, took a small box from hers and put it into Charlotte's. "That sounds familiar, too, but you never know."

"What are you doing? What did you put in my purse?"

"A package of condoms."

"*What?*"

Renee winked. "It wouldn't hurt to be prepared."

Charlotte moved her hands to her cheeks and stared at her sister. The quick thud of her pulse had to be from embarrassment, right?

Renee pulled her hands down and squeezed her fingers. "We've all seen the sparks between the two of you. I think something is already happening. It probably never really stopped."

Genevieve's laughter drifted through the curtain, mingling with Jackson's deep voice. From the sound of things, he and Pete were debating the definition of jazz with her. It all seemed so ordinary and comfortable, Charlotte was surprised to feel the sting of tears. "Jackson and I were barely more than children when we dated, Renee," she said finally. "I admit I have a fondness for the boy I knew, but we've both grown up and moved on."

"The important things don't change, Charlotte. When Pete came back into my life, I hadn't thought there was any chance for the two of us. There were so many problems to work through, I wasn't sure I wanted to try. I'm glad we did."

"And I'm happy for you, Renee. I think it's wonderful that you found someone to love. I'm happy for Sylvie, Melanie and Mama, too. But please, leave this alone."

"Charlotte—"

"You're right that the important things don't change, and that includes our problems. Jackson and I were wrong for each other twenty years ago and we still are."

"Are you sure?"

"I love you for caring." She stretched to kiss Renee's cheek, then looked at the blue gown that gleamed from the rack of costumes. "But this is real life, not a fairy tale. No one's going to wave a magic wand and…"

Her words trailed off. The feathers that trimmed the gown were stirring on some current of air that Charlotte couldn't feel, setting off a flash of sequins that made the costume appear to be winking at her.

And for a heartbeat she saw an image of herself wearing that gown in front of an ivy-cloaked castle as she danced with a man whose dusky blue eyes were an exact match for the color of the satin.

In the fairy tale, Sleeping Beauty had been awakened by a kiss.

Jackson had kissed her that morning.

But that hadn't been a real kiss. It had been too light and too short. He'd barely touched her lips with his.

Yet his taste still lingered. And the sound of his voice from the next room gave her pleasant little tingles. And her pulse did a shimmy every time she thought of him spending another night so close that she could almost hear him breathing.

Something *had* changed with that kiss. Not an awakening as much as a shift in perception.

But that wasn't magic. It was hormones and proximity, a normal physical reaction between an emotionally strung out woman and an incredibly attractive, sensitive and sexy man. She was far too sensible to attribute her feelings to anything else.

At what point did rationalization become denial?

The thought made her groan, but she managed to catch herself before she began massaging her temples again. Keeping her gaze firmly averted from the fairy-tale dress, she slipped on her jacket, picked up her purse and followed Renee from the room.

MIKE DRUMMED HIS fingers against the armrest of the limo, watching as the two couples left the building. The place wasn't far from his syrup company's warehouse, but he'd had no reason to take notice of it before. It was nothing but a small costume store, sandwiched between a pawnshop and a boarded-up space that had once held a dry cleaner's. Like countless businesses in the city, it relied on the seasonal income from Mardi Gras, so its profits would be too unreliable for Mike to demand a piece.

Still, the store would have been a good location for an ambush. The street was a long way from the crowds of the French Quarter, and anyone who was around would know enough to mind their own business. The old cripple who ran the store wouldn't have presented any problem either. With two of the Marchand sisters in the same place at once, he could have gotten more bang for his buck.

But he'd have to wait for another opportunity. The men who had accompanied the women to the costume store didn't look as if they'd scare easily. He'd seen Pete Traynor before—the idiot Corbins had gotten him stirred up when they'd staged a hit-and-run that had injured his nephew. It had been a foolhardy risk, as reckless as Richard's half-baked attempt a week ago to abduct Anne Marchand. They'd been lucky their whole scheme hadn't blown up in their faces. The Corbins would have been no use to him if they'd ended up in jail.

When Mike made his move, he would be leaving nothing to chance. Especially the cops. He pointed to the dark-haired man who walked beside Charlotte. "Who's that guy in the denim jacket, Otis? I saw him with that Marchand woman on Thursday, too."

Detective Otis Fergusson squinted toward the window, then folded his hands over his bulk and resettled against the padded seat across from Mike. "His name's Jackson Bailey. He's a hotshot surgeon visiting from Philadelphia. He seems to be an old friend of the family."

Mike accepted the information with a nod. Putting Otis on his payroll had been one of the smartest moves he'd made.

His relationship with the New Orleans detective had started decades ago, when Mike had been fresh from the bayou and starting up a numbers racket in Algiers. Otis had been only a beat cop then and he'd been happy to look the other way in exchange for an envelope of cash. As the amount in the envelope had increased, so had the cop's usefulness.

Things had progressed from there to a mutually beneficial financial arrangement that had lasted longer than any of Mike's marriages. And like any good marriage, Mike's relationship with Otis was exclusive. Even the Corbins weren't aware that Otis was working for him.

"I interviewed Bailey a few days ago," Otis continued. "He was the first one to suggest I speak to the Corbins about the trouble at the hotel."

"Are you sure he's only a doctor?"

"I checked him out. He's one of those do-gooders who work in disaster zones. Real straight shooter. You're not going to like this, but he's certain that Luc Carter was trying to put out the fire your people started."

Mike frowned. So his suspicions about Carter's nervousness that night had been well-founded. "The Corbins might have been right. Carter doesn't have any guts."

"It could be more than that. He could be growing a conscience."

"Why? Did he spill something when you interviewed him?"

"No, but I did some digging into Carter's background since then. It took me a while to uncover the connection—I found out he's related to the Marchands."

Mike didn't like being surprised. The Corbins hadn't told him this, so either they didn't know or they weren't being completely straight with him. Neither possibility was good. His frown deepened. "How's he related?"

"Carter's old man was Anne Marchand's brother. He was the black sheep, got kicked out of the family when he was a kid."

"So Luc Carter is Anne Marchand's nephew," Mike said slowly, digesting the information. "And those sisters are his cousins."

"Yeah, only they don't know. It's just a guess, but I'd say Carter made his deal with the Corbins out of revenge. He's probably looking to bring his family down as payback for how they treated his father."

"And you're sure the Marchands don't know who he is?"

"Positive. He's been going by his mother's maiden name so they wouldn't know—"

"Wait a minute." Mike leaned forward. "You said his father was Anne Marchand's brother? What was his name?"

"Pierre Robichaux."

As the pieces began to click into place, Mike was startled into a sudden laugh. "Pierre Robichaux? Damn, that's rich."

"Why?"

"I knew him. He was one of my best customers and he never caught on that the games were rigged. He ran up close to a million in markers...." Mike smiled and relaxed against the seat cushion, enjoying the irony of the situation. If Carter was going after the Marchands to avenge his father, he was looking in the wrong direction.

"Do you want me to take Carter out?" Otis asked.

Mike considered that for a while, then shook his head. "I don't want to get rid of him yet. His connection to the Marchands is going to make him an easy fall guy. Once the plan goes down, you can shoot him in the line of duty. We'll make sure to plant enough incriminating evidence to get you a commendation."

A deep chuckle rumbled from Otis's belly. To someone who didn't know him the way Mike did, the laugh would sound jolly. "I can use one," Otis said. "My captain's been on my back about this case since the Marchands started questioning people about the fire. It looks as if they're trying to run their own investigation."

"You can handle it, can't you?"

"No problem. They're not going to find any evidence, I guarantee it."

Mike flipped open the compartment beneath the seat beside him and handed Otis his payment for the week.

The envelope was continuing to get fatter, but the cop had earned every penny.

THE CRAMPED RESEARCH lab on the top floor of Tulane's medical building was silent apart from the *snick-click* of the computer keyboard Dr. Yves Fortier hunched over and the muted beeps as the machine registered another reading. Yves' wife, Marie, hovered beside the table where Jackson was seated, her brow creased in concentration as she monitored his pulse and the current that was going through his hand.

Charlotte understood the procedure wasn't painful, but it would be uncomfortable. Tiny pads with electronic sensors had been placed over every millimeter of Jackson's hand, trailing fine wires that bristled outward like a bizarre metal glove. One by one and then in carefully determined sequences each electrode was stimulated and the level of response to the charge was recorded. The data was being fed into a computer program that would build a three-dimensional map of the wound and the degree of damage to the affected nerves.

Watching the slow, methodical process was frustrating for her, so she could imagine how agonizing this must be for Jackson. Every tingle he felt—and especially every tingle he didn't feel—was like the vote of a jury that would determine his fate. She could see his tension in the stiff set of his shoulders and the angle of his jaw, yet each time he met her gaze, he managed a smile.

He'd warned her the tests could be lengthy and had been prepared to leave her at the hotel and come back for her when they were done, yet she hadn't considered letting him go through this alone. Lending him moral support was the least she could do, given how generously he was involving himself in her problems.

She shifted on her chair, uncomfortable with the excuses she was continuing to make. Her reasons for being here weren't that unselfish. In spite of what she'd told Renee, and all the warnings she tried to give herself, she wanted to be here. She liked being around Jackson, regardless of why.

She liked his friends, too. Yves and Marie had greeted him like a brother. Their affection had shone through Yves' gruff joking and Marie's bossy instructions as she'd helped position the equipment. They'd been surprised to see Charlotte but had accepted her presence with good grace, happily finding her a spot in the corner where she could remain without getting in the way.

The husband-and-wife team appeared to be in their fifties and worked together with the ease of lifelong partners. They reminded Charlotte of her parents, since their careers had meshed with their marriage. Unlike her parents, though, the Fortiers had no children, so they were both free to travel the world, dedicating their time to helping others. Their relationship had worked because they shared the same goal and the same dream.

And if the looks they exchanged were any indication, they also shared a deep tenderness for each other.

How different might things have been if Charlotte had gone with Jackson twenty years ago instead of choosing to marry Adrian and build her life here? What if she hadn't loved the hotel or wanted children and if the bonds of her family and her roots hadn't held her in New Orleans? Would she and Jackson have ended up as comfortable and in love as the Fortiers?

The questions were pointless—she couldn't change the past. If she'd made a different choice, she probably would have grown to resent Jackson. Giving up her own dreams would have led to bitterness. She couldn't change who she was any more than Jackson could have changed.

Yves rolled his stool a few feet back from the keyboard and stretched his arms over his head. "That's enough for tonight, Jacques," he said. "Marie, you can go ahead and turn off the gizmos."

Marie flipped a switch, and the low hum that had been vibrating in the floor ceased. She patted Jackson's arm. "I don't see what Yves was complaining about. You're a wonderful patient."

Yves snorted and glanced from Marie to Charlotte. "He's always on his best behavior around beautiful women."

"That's a fact," Jackson said. He began plucking the sensors from his hand. "Beautiful women bring out the best in any man."

"Ah, so that's why you're still a bachelor," Yves said.

"How's that?"

"There are times when a woman prefers a man to behave badly." Yves winked. "Isn't that right, Marie?"

Laughing, Marie walked over to her husband and gave him a swat. "I don't know why I tolerate you."

"Because I'm a genius, of course. That's what Jacques said."

"Genius?" Marie asked. "Since when?"

"I was smart enough to marry you, wasn't I?"

Jackson smiled at their banter as he continued to remove the sensors. Charlotte rose from her chair and went over to help him lay the wires flat on the table as he pulled them off. "How are you feeling?" she asked.

"Better ask Yves," he said. "That was the whole point of this exercise."

Despite the smile he was giving his friends, Charlotte could see the tightness in Jackson's movements. She smoothed the final wire on the table and looked at Yves.

"It's too soon to say for certain." Yves slid off his stool and rolled it back underneath the computer keyboard, then gave an elaborate shrug. "These toys need more time to process the results completely."

Jackson reached for a cloth to wipe off the gel that had held the electrodes in place. He kept his gaze on his fingers. "What are your findings so far then?"

Yves looked at Marie. It was only a quick glance, but Charlotte recognized the private communication of sympathy between them. She knew immediately that the results wouldn't be what any of them were hoping for.

No! she thought. This had to work out. She took the cloth from Jackson, lifted his hand and gently wiped off the gel that still gleamed from his knuckles. From the top, the wound looked too minor to be serious. It was still hard to believe that the damage could be permanent.

"Many of the readings were inconclusive," Yves hedged.

Jackson put his good hand over Charlotte's, stilling her movements. "So it's bad, huh?"

"Jacques..." Yves sighed. "As your friend, I am tempted to lie. But as your colleague, I respect you too much to do so. Yes, it is bad."

Jackson took the cloth from Charlotte's grasp and tossed it on the table, then got to his feet and shrugged on his jacket. Rather than stepping back, she moved closer to his side until her shoulder pressed against his chest, silently using the contact of their bodies to express her support.

A hush fell over the lab as he slid his arm around her waist. "What about the possible bone fragments you talked about the other day, Yves?" he asked. "You could go in and clean them out."

"If there were more than what I saw on the X-rays, your body would already have incorporated them into the scar tissue. The damage is done. They'll dissolve eventually, but if I intervene now, it's more likely that you could lose the nerve function you've managed to recover."

Jackson tightened his hold on Charlotte. "Could you run the test again, Yves?"

"I could, but—"

"*Absolument,*" Marie interrupted, giving her husband another swat. "We shall not give up yet. These toys my genius is so fond of only measure what technology designed them to measure, so they are not infallible."

Yves pursed his lips, then blew out his breath noisily and gave a vigorous nod. "Marie is right. It won't hurt to double-check the data. Come back on Tuesday and we'll try it once more."

"And in the meantime," Marie said, "I have something that will help." She took a flat palm-size, paper-wrapped package from a bookshelf near the door and held it out to Jackson. "This is for you."

Jackson regarded the package skeptically. "Let me guess. Is that the gris-gris Yves prescribed?"

Marie smiled as she slipped the package into the breast pocket of his jacket. "I know you don't believe, Jacques, but keep it anyway." She patted his pocket. "There are some aspects to healing that no science can explain."

CHAPTER EIGHT

JACKSON WANTED A DRINK. No, not just one drink, a whole bottle. And he wanted good, honest, burn-your-gut whiskey, not the wimpy white wine that sat in Charlotte's refrigerator. Something that would guarantee him oblivion fast with the least amount of effort.

He muttered an oath and tightened his grip on the open fridge door. The motor clicked on, chugging out a sobering stream of cold air. He ducked his head and inhaled deeply. He knew that avoiding a problem wouldn't solve it. And as tempting as it might be, this was no time to crawl into an alcoholic stupor.

It had only been one test, he reminded himself, and technology wasn't always reliable. He'd seen false test results before. It might have been a long shot to ask Yves to run the procedure again, yet even bad odds were better than nothing. As long as there was the slimmest hope, Jackson had to keep trying.

But it was getting damned hard not to give up. When did hope cross the line into denial?

He swung the door shut, rattling the bottle against the metal shelf and plunging the kitchen into darkness. Instead of turning on a light, he gave his vision a few moments to adjust, then walked past the table to the window. Folding his arms over his chest, he looked out at the shadowed yard.

Giving up wasn't an option. Not for him. And not for Charlotte either.

She was the other reason he couldn't indulge himself by getting drunk. He'd promised to help watch over her. The hotel security people had assured him the alarm system in this house was a good one, and he'd followed their advice and checked that the windows were locked and the doors were dead-bolted, but it would be dangerous to put himself out of commission. The Corbins had been lying low for two days now, so they were bound to try something else soon. He couldn't afford to lower his guard.

A few shafts of moonlight glinted through the leaves, speckling the small patio with patches of silver. The riot of light and color he'd seen this morning when Charlotte had stood here was gone. The scene was no longer inviting. It wasn't only because the light was different, it was because the woman who had made it seem special wasn't here.

When it came to Charlotte, he'd already lowered his guard. All those warnings he'd tried to give himself about not getting close to her hadn't worked. He was far too accustomed to her presence. Just having her stand next to him tonight had made Yves' words easier to bear.

He'd managed fine on his own for half his lifetime, yet the more time he spent with Charlotte, the more his old feelings stirred. She'd been his friend and ally as well as his girlfriend. He'd almost forgotten how good it felt to know that someone cared.

And she did care. He could see it in her eyes and feel it in her touch. It wasn't the reckless infatuation they'd shared as teenagers, though. She was a mature, intelligent woman, as cautious as he was.

Yet her caution was good, right? Otherwise…

"Can't you sleep?"

At the sound of her voice, his pulse leaped. Seeing her now was the last thing he needed.

Yet it was exactly what he wanted. He turned his head toward the doorway.

She was silhouetted against the darkened hall, a pale, ankle-length robe wrapped around her body. Like him, she was barefoot, which was probably why he hadn't heard her approach. With her hair loose around her shoulders and her eyes gleaming in the faint light that seeped through the window she looked as if she'd just risen from her bed.

The desire that spread through him was no surprise. In one form or another it had been building all day. It was another reason he could have used a drink. "That's right," he said. "Sorry if I woke you up."

"You didn't." She tightened the belt of her robe, and the fabric rippled with the sensuous gleam of silk. If she was wearing anything underneath, it couldn't be much.

Jackson gritted his teeth and stayed where he was. He was grateful now that he had taken the time to pull on his jeans. As it was, he could swear he felt her gaze move across his bare chest as if she were touching him. "Did you want something?"

"I was about to ask you the same question. There's some wine in the fridge."

"I saw it."

"You're welcome to have some."

"It wouldn't help the situation, Charlotte."

"Maybe it would help if you talked about it."

"There's nothing to talk about."

"That sounds like what I said last week." She walked to the stove and switched on the light above it. A soft glow pooled around her, leaving the rest of the room in shadow. "Next are you going to tell me that it's none of my business?"

"Charlotte—"

"I do know what you're going through, Jackson," she said.

Yes, she did, he thought. Her quiet sympathy felt as good now as it had in Yves' lab.

"It's tough to be what everyone expects you to be," she added.

He lowered the blind over the window and leaned his back against the frame. The color of her robe was the same vibrant green hue as her eyes, only a few shades paler. It shimmered as she moved, drawing his gaze to her body. "And what's that?"

"Strong. Responsible." She opened and closed a few cupboards as if she were looking for something. "Perfect."

He shook his head. "You were the one who had to live up to everyone's expectations, not me. No one ever expected me to be perfect. I was the poor kid who wasn't supposed to amount to anything."

"That's not true. I never thought of you like that."

"Maybe you didn't, but others did."

"If by others you mean *Grand-mère*, I'd say you proved her wrong years ago." She leaned over to open a cupboard beside the stove. There was a rattle of pots.

Jackson tried to keep his gaze off her rear end, but the way that silk tightened over her buttocks was impossible to ignore. "What are you doing?"

She straightened up and turned to face him with a small saucepan in her hand. "I'm making some hot chocolate."

"You're kidding."

Her lips quirked. "I realize I told you I don't cook, but this is one thing I should be able to manage."

Jackson shifted, pushing away from the window frame. She wasn't wearing any makeup, yet her cheeks were tinted with a soft blush. Without lipstick, her mouth looked lush and much too kissable. "I remember. You used to make that after school sometimes."

"It might help you sleep."

It was the middle of the night, he was half-naked and alone with a desirable woman. Sleep was the furthest thing from his mind right now. So was chocolate.

But indulging himself with Charlotte would be almost as bad as getting drunk.

Then again, he would probably feel a hell of a lot better in the morning if he woke up with her instead of a hangover. He'd gone into her bedroom each time he'd checked the windows. Unlike the rest of the furniture in this house, that big brass bed of hers would have plenty of space for both of them. He could all too easily imagine stretching out on it with Charlotte in his arms, her hair sliding across his chest, her silk robe on the floor...

He grabbed a chair, reversed it and straddled the seat. *Think of something else*, he ordered himself. He glanced at the fax machine on the table—as usual, there was a fresh sheaf of faxes in front of it. "Has Renee heard anything more from the EMS personnel about the fire?"

"Yes, she got several more statements. It appears that some

people don't think much of Detective Fergusson. Everyone's being very cooperative."

"What about that insurance agent? Manning."

"He's still not accepting my calls." She took a carton of milk from the fridge, then hunted through the cupboards again until she came up with the chocolate and sugar. "I can't blame him. Until we can get the official report changed, he wouldn't be able to pay out. The insurance companies took a hit after Katrina that they're still recovering from."

"So did the hotel," he said. "That's why you're in this financial fix anyway, isn't it?"

She put the pot on the stove and adjusted the heat. It was a while before she replied. "Our problems started a few years before the hurricane, Jackson."

"How?"

"It was around the time of my father's accident."

"I'm sorry about Remy, Charlotte. He was a good man."

"Yes, he was, and I loved him dearly. But for some reason he liquidated a substantial part of the family's savings and transferred the money to the Cayman Islands just before he died."

He tried to hide his shock. Remy Marchand had been one of the most honest, ethical businessmen Jackson had ever known. What was more, the man had been completely devoted to his wife and daughters. He was the last person who would be involved in something shady.

Yet what legitimate reason could he have had to take funds from his family and transfer them to a notorious tax haven?

Charlotte kept her gaze on the pot as she continued to speak. "We didn't discover the money was gone until after the funeral. At first we thought it was an accounting mistake, but the paper trail was indisputable. We still have no idea why Papa did that, but knowing him, he must have had a good reason."

"I'm sure he did."

"He probably meant the transfer to be temporary. He wouldn't have willingly left us in financial difficulty. But we had to spend the bulk of our reserve funds to keep the hotel going after the hurricane, so the loss of that million hit us hard."

"Did you say *million?*"

She nodded. "That's why we're mortgaged to the limit. There's no more safety net. If we don't turn a profit by next week, we'll have to worry about the banks more than the Corbins."

He thought about that for a while. It was still difficult for him to grasp how far the Marchands had fallen. When he'd been a kid, their wealth had seemed unlimited.

"I try to be sensible, Jackson, because you're right— that's what everyone expects of me. But it's hard not to get discouraged."

"Yeah, it is hard."

"The theme of our Mardi Gras ball this year is fairy tales. My family's really getting into it." Although she kept her voice level, her hand trembled as she took the pot from the stove. "It probably sounds silly to you, but sometimes I almost wish I did still believe in magic so it could solve our problems. God knows, I've tried everything else."

He folded his arms on the back of the chair. "I know what you mean. It sure would be simpler if Marie's gris-gris worked."

"I'd forgotten about that. Where did you put it?"

"It's probably still in my jacket pocket. I don't want to throw it out—it would hurt her feelings."

"Same with me. I'd prefer not to go through the motions

of the ball, but my family's counting on me, and our customers are looking forward to it." She tipped the pot to pour the steaming chocolate into two mugs. "But I wish I hadn't agreed to that fairy-tale theme—"

Her words cut off on a gasp. She jerked backward and the pot clunked to the floor, spattering the remainder of the chocolate.

Jackson sprang from his chair and crossed the kitchen in two strides. He caught her arm to steady her. "Charlotte?"

She pulled free from his grip to shove her fingertips into her mouth.

It was easy to put the clues together. "You burned yourself."

Her shoulders shook as she nodded. "Mmph!"

"Let me take a look," he said, grasping her wrist.

She popped her fingers from her mouth. "It's nothing. Really."

He led her closer to the light over the stove so that he could study her hand. The skin at the tips of her first and second fingers was slightly reddened, but that was all. It didn't look serious enough to blister. "We'll run some cold water over the burn," he said, guiding her to the sink. "That should help."

She straightened her fingers to hold the tips under the stream of cold water. Although she didn't appear to be in pain, the trembling in her shoulders spread to her hand.

Concerned, Jackson shut off the water and looked at her face.

Her lips were clamped tightly together, yet the corners of her mouth were twitching uncontrollably. Her eyes were brimming, not with tears but with amusement. The moment she met his gaze, the laughter burst free.

The sound filled the kitchen as easily as sunlight, washing over his bare skin, warming his blood faster than any whiskey could have.

God, how long had it been since he'd heard her laugh like that? It wasn't elegant or ladylike and wouldn't belong in her grandmother's parlor. No, it wasn't a laugh to go with good manners and tea. It was full-out and honest, a sound that came from her heart. He used to love it.

He still did.

"This," she said, waving her wet fingers, "this is what I get for even mentioning magic."

"What?"

"Something seems to go wrong whenever I do." She looked at the pot. "This is also why I don't cook."

He grinned. "Your intentions were good."

"But not my aim," she said, her voice breaking as she started into another laugh. She shook her head, pressing her hand over her mouth.

Jackson tugged her hand free. "Don't stop," he said. "That laugh is the best thing I've heard in years. We both need this."

"Laugh therapy?"

"Why not?"

"We must be cracking up from stress," she mumbled. "Spilling chocolate isn't that funny and I still have to clean the mess."

"I'll help you."

"But it's all over the cupboards and the floor."

"Uh-huh. You always were very thorough when you took on a task."

She gasped for breath and shoved her hair from her forehead. Her laughter subsided to giggles. "That's me, all right. The Marchand overachiever. I take every disaster seriously."

He chuckled. "You've got some on yourself, too."

She glanced down at her robe. A cluster of dark droplets spattered the silk over her right breast. "Great. I'll have to—"

"Allow me." Jackson licked the pad of his thumb and pressed it over one of the spots.

"Jackson!"

He could hear the caution in her voice, but it didn't quite drown out the remnants of her laughter. He could feel it quivering through her breast.

The moment could go either way, he thought. It wasn't too late to drop his hand, step back and shrug this off. No big deal, just one of those things. Keep the mood playful and casual, get a mop, clean the kitchen and get the hell away from her.

But the heat of her skin was making his pulse thud. And less than an inch from the edge of his thumbnail he could see the outline of her nipple. It was swelling as he watched, puckering the pale green silk in a way that no red-blooded man could ignore.

"Jackson?"

He lifted his thumb and spread his fingers, holding his palm a whisper above her breast, not touching anymore yet near enough for him to feel her warmth. "Yes?"

The word hung on the air. It was less a reply than it was a question.

Charlotte met his gaze squarely, her eyes sparkling with the same honesty that had powered her laughter. The aroma of the spilled chocolate drifted around them. The stove element ticked as it cooled. Other than that, the moment stretched out in silence.

Somehow Jackson managed to hold himself motionless in spite of the demands that were surging through his body. He used every shred of self-control he possessed to leave the choice of what happened next up to her.

They both knew she could have easily stepped back.

Instead she leaned forward and pressed herself into his hand.

Charlotte moaned in delight as Jackson closed his fingers around her breast, drowning out the voice of reason that was jabbering in her head. She wasn't going to listen. This felt too good. Even better than the laughter.

Warmth radiated from Jackson's palm. The thin robe and the nightgown she wore beneath it presented little barrier to his touch. He explored her slowly, squeezing gently with his fingers, rubbing lightly with the heel of his hand, letting the silk slide over her in a caress of its own. And just as she began to sway, light-headed from the pleasure, he anchored his free arm behind her waist and rolled the tip of his thumb over her nipple.

She shuddered and clutched his shoulders, arching her back in a silent request for more.

He smiled, bringing the hint of a boyish dimple to one cheek and deepening the sexy grooves beside his mouth. He moved his hand to her other breast, treating it to the same thoroughness.

There was familiarity in his touch, yet it was flavored with discovery. It was as if they were doing this for the first time all over again.

Charlotte was surprised that she felt no shyness—it had been a very long time since any man had touched her this way—yet this was Jackson, the person who had once known her better than anyone in the world. It felt more than good, it felt right.

Her lips curved with anticipation as she slid her hands down his arms. She lingered over the lean ridges of his biceps, reveling in the fine tremor that followed her touch. She'd been wanting to touch him since she'd walked into the room and seen him standing beside the window. Hadn't he realized how appealing he looked with his hair in a tangle and his feet bare and those jeans riding low on his hips? His chest was magnificent, broad and taut and perfectly tapered. She splayed her fingers in the center, enjoying the crisp hair that sprang back against her hands.

Not for one second did she confuse him with a boy—she was exceedingly grateful that he was all grown up. Smiling, she followed the dark line that led to his navel. It was only then that she realized he hadn't fastened the stud on the waistband of his jeans.

She focused on the open stud and then the naked skin and hint of black hair that showed behind it. He wasn't wearing underwear. Her gaze dropped lower. Heat rushed to her cheeks, her belly and her thighs.

He cupped the back of her neck. "Charlotte?"

She looked up. Tension hardened his jaw. At the base of his throat she could see his pulse racing.

It was another moment when things could go either way. It still wasn't too late. Going further wasn't smart. It was crazy. Pointless.

But as she already knew, there had never been anything logical about their relationship, had there? Moistening her lips, she hooked her fingers in his waistband.

His breathing changed, growing ragged. Frank arousal shone in his eyes as he gave her a smile that sent a thrill clear down to her toes. Holding her gaze, he eased her back over his arm. Then he lowered his head and licked the drops of chocolate from her robe.

If it had started as a game, it wasn't one now. She could feel his tongue through the silk. The moistened fabric clung to her skin as he moved his mouth over her, increasing the friction, heightening the sensation in a way that was more erotic than if she'd been naked. He took his time, working his way to her throat and the special spot beneath the corner of her jaw where his kiss used to make her shudder.

It still did. Within minutes she was shaking with need. She dug her nails into his back, her breath coming in sharp bursts. "Jackson…" She tunneled her fingers into his hair and lifted his head. "Jackson, please."

He straightened up, pulled her with him and answered her plea with a kiss. It was unlike any they'd shared before. There was nothing tentative or gentle about it. Hard and hot, he stroked his tongue against hers and clamped his hand on her buttocks. Fitting her to his body, he slipped his leg between her thighs, triggering a response that took the strength from her knees. Before she could fall, he wrapped his arms around her waist, lifted her off the floor and backed her across the room.

Her shoulders hit the wall beside the doorway, driving her body into his with a pleasure so intense it bordered on pain. Trembling, she reached down to grab her robe and her nightgown and yanked the fabric up to her waist. A zipper rasped. Denim slid against her most sensitive skin. Jackson shifted to brace his legs apart and held her against the wall with the weight of his body. Straining, breathless, she tilted her hips to meet him.

This was like nothing they'd shared before either. It was wild and raw, sex at its most basic. Instinct took over as she matched his rhythm stroke for stroke, savoring his thrusts and reveling in his strength. Passion built past the point of reason….

Charlotte never realized when she closed her eyes and gave herself up to the magic.

CHAPTER NINE

SHE AWOKE TO THE smell of coffee. Charlotte opened one eye groggily and squinted at the steaming mug that sat on the trunk beside her bed. Her eyelids felt stiff. So did every joint in her body. She couldn't remember fixing coffee already. She must have fallen back to sleep again. Maybe it was time to cut back on the caffeine. Or at least get a new mattress.

"Good morning, Charlie."

Her eyes flew open. "Jackson?"

The mattress dipped, rolling her onto her back. Jackson knelt beside her hip and smiled. "How are you feeling?"

She was never at her best when she first woke up, but the fuzziness of her brain now wasn't due to the time of day, it was because of Jackson. The sight of a man like that in her bedroom would muddle any woman's mind.

His hair was wet, combed back from his forehead and firmly in place for a change. The skin on his jaw had the unique gleam that followed a fresh shave. He'd put on his pants, but his shirt was still unbuttoned, the sides hanging loose against his chest. The scent of soap and warm early-morning male drifted through her senses. It was far more stimulating than coffee.

She groaned and put her forearm over her eyes. She needed time to think.

"It's hard to be logical when we're having this conversation in bed."

"I can't think of a better place to have it." He moved his finger from her lips to her neck, then traced his way along her jaw to the base of her ear. "We're two consenting adults with some exceptional physical chemistry. Why shouldn't we relax and enjoy what we've got?"

Once again she couldn't think of a reason to protest. Being responsible and sensible had never left her feeling *this* good.

So why shouldn't they enjoy themselves? He was right. Maybe she had been making this too complicated. She and Jackson were adults, not idealistic kids with false expectations. That's what had led to the pain in the past. It was different now. They knew what they both wanted and they were being realistic. What harm would there be....

Oh, she couldn't think when he touched her like that. She trailed her hand along his arm. "As long as we're clear that what happened was just sex."

He pressed closer and slid his leg over hers. "Well, it wasn't *just* sex."

"No?"

"It was curl-your-toes-and-singe-your-eyebrows sex."

She laughed. "We're certainly better at it than we used to be."

He dropped his forehead against her shoulder. "In my defense, I was just a horny teenager. I didn't know what I was doing back then."

She laid her cheek against his damp hair, engulfed by a wave of memories. She and Jackson had lost their virginity together. In spite of all the hand-holding and necking they had done when they'd dated, she'd been a good girl, so she'd made him wait until after they had graduated high school before she'd agreed to go "all the way."

It hadn't been the romantic rapture she'd expected. They'd been too young and naive to know what they were doing. Their first encounter had been on a stack of blankets in the back of his father's delivery van. It had been furtive, painful and a crashing disappointment. The subsequent attempts had embarrassed him and frustrated her. But before they'd found the opportunity to practice, he'd gone off to college. Still trying to cling to her fantasy of romance, she had decided to save any further intimacy for their wedding night.

Of course, as it had turned out, she hadn't ended up marrying Jackson. But her response to physical intimacy had never gotten much better. It was only natural that she would assume the problem lay with her.

She stroked his back, spreading her fingers as she followed the ridges of his shoulder blades. "Neither of us knew what we were doing back then, Jackson."

"But we do now."

Was that what made the difference? Were they simply more skilled? More likely it was because of all the stress they'd been under recently, just as he'd said.

They had both really, *really* needed this.

Something that felt suspiciously like a giggle rose in her throat. "I suppose."

He lifted his head and looked at her. "You suppose? Want to see the scratches you gave me?"

Smiling, she reached up to push back the hair that had fallen over his forehead—once it dried, there would be no keeping it in place. "Are you fishing for compliments?"

He touched his fingertips to the corner of her mouth. "No, that smile speaks for itself."

"Uh-huh." She licked the side of his finger. "And what does it say?"

"Hang on, I'd better get a second opinion." He grasped the edge of the sheet and eased it downward, then whistled softly at what he'd revealed. "Why, Miss Charlotte, I do believe you're shouting."

She stretched her arms over her head, luxuriating in his regard. She still hadn't touched her coffee, yet her body was awakening at a record pace.

He stroked his knuckle along the underside of her breast. "You've grown, you know."

"Have I?"

"Oh, yeah. Ripened. Filled out. You're a beautiful woman, Charlie."

Blood began to pulse in every tender area. Stress, need, whatever she wanted to call it, it was happening again. She shifted her hips so she could put her hand on his thigh. "You've changed, too."

"I've grown bigger?"

She could tell by his smile what he wanted to hear, so she decided to tease him. "You're hairier."

He slid on top of her, then leaned back on his heels to straddle her thighs. "Is there anything else you happened to notice?"

"You're, uh, slower."

A deep chuckle rumbled from his chest. "I should hope so."

She sat up and slipped her hands under his shirt. "What time is it?"

"Almost seven. What time do you need to be at the hotel?"

"My first appointment isn't until ten."

"That gives us—" He stopped. "Damn!"

"What's wrong?"

He kissed her forehead, then eased backward, away from her touch. "I wasn't prepared for what happened last night, but we can't take any more chances. I need to find a drugstore."

It took her a second to realize he was talking about birth control. It was lucky that he'd remembered—why hadn't she thought of it herself? Her brain really was having trouble functioning when it came to this man. She caught the edges of his shirt before he could retreat further. "Check my purse. It's in the living room."

"Your purse?"

"Renee gave me a box of condoms yesterday."

Jackson hadn't slowed down that much after all, Charlotte decided, laughing as he sprinted through the doorway.

JACKSON HOOKED HIS heel on a rung of the bar stool, unconsciously moving his head and shoulders in time to the beat that wove through the jazz. He'd heard that the woman who was singing, Holly Carlyle, used to perform regularly here at the Hotel Marchand until she'd started to sing in her boyfriend's club, but in the party spirit of Mardi Gras, she was putting in a guest appearance tonight. The show was a treat—Holly's vocals were pure, easy and perfectly in tune with the mellow tones of the saxophone that played in the background.

And speaking of being in tune… Jackson moved his gaze to the table where Charlotte sat. Although she was immersed in her conversation with Melanie, her foot was keeping time with the beat. He liked the look of her in those high heels. They made her legs look sexy and gave a little wiggle to her walk. He liked her habit of wearing skirts rather than pants, too. She'd left the tailored suit jacket and blouse at home today and had worn a sweater instead. To someone who didn't know her, the beige cashmere might seem conservative, almost bland, giving no hint of the passionate woman it masked.

As if she felt his regard, she turned her head to meet his gaze. Her eyes sparkled in a brief private smile before she returned her attention to her sister.

That was all it took for his body to respond. He shifted to find a more comfortable position on his stool, his mouth lifting wryly at his lack of control. He would have thought after those hours in her bed this morning his desire would have started to wane. Instead it was only getting stronger. He might not be a teenager anymore, but he still had the appetite of one.

He wouldn't have guessed that he and Charlotte would be so compatible in bed, considering how disastrous their teenage attempts at sex had been. On the other hand, the circumstances they found themselves in were exceptional. As he'd reasoned earlier, given their current situation, they'd both benefited from physical release. In fact, it was healthy.

What had he been so worried about? It was sex, that's all. He wasn't going to open any old wounds. And he sure as hell wasn't going to make the mistake of falling in love with Charlotte Marchand again.

At the thought, his smile faded. No, he wouldn't fall in love. It wasn't part of the equation this time. They were both clear about why they were together—he was helping her get through the next few days, that was all.

Jackson did a slow survey of the barroom, noting the uniformed security guards near the entrances. Several more who weren't wearing uniforms blended in with the crowd. As he looked past the door to the service corridor, he saw a tall man walk through and head purposefully toward Charlotte's table. Jackson didn't try to intercept him—it was Robert LeSoeur. The women had been waiting for him to arrive so they could discuss the refreshments for Tuesday night's ball.

Robert sat beside Melanie and draped his arm across the back of her chair. He didn't try to hide how he felt about the youngest Marchand sister. The love on his face was obvious, and why not? Those two shared the same profession. They worked in the same place and had the same goals. They were obviously well suited for each other. Neither one was expected to give up anything for the other.

But he wasn't going to open old wounds, Jackson reminded himself.

"Sorry, Luc. I think you've had enough."

Jackson looked toward the voice. The pair of customers who had occupied the stools beside him had departed, giving him a clear view of the man who sat at the end of the bar.

It was Luc Carter, the hotel's concierge. He was still wearing his uniform blazer, but the knot of his tie hung loosely and his shirt collar was unbuttoned. His normally neat blond hair was furrowed, as if he'd been raking his hands through it. He rapped his empty glass against the bar. "I haven't had anywhere near enough, Leo. Give me another."

"I'm trying to do you a favor, man," the bartender said, easing the empty glass from his hand. "You want to make an ass of yourself in front of the boss? Miss Charlotte is right over there."

Luc twisted to look behind him and nearly tipped off his stool. He grabbed the edge of the bar to retain his balance. "Come on, I finished my shift. Just one more."

Jackson moved down the bar and sat beside Luc. "How's your wrist?"

Luc blinked to focus on him, his eyelids sluggish. "Fine, doc. Couldn't be better."

The scent of alcohol on Luc's breath confirmed what his disheveled appearance and lack of coordination had already made apparent. It was no wonder the bartender had refused to serve him—this man appeared to be as drunk as Jackson had been tempted to get the night before.

Jackson glanced at Leo. "A black coffee, please," he said quietly. He waited until the bartender brought the cup, then tapped his finger against Luc's sleeve near the place where he'd bandaged the cut. "Has anyone looked at this since the night of the fire?"

"I told you, it's fine."

Keeping his movements casual, Jackson slid the sleeve back until he saw the edge of a clean gauze bandage. He touched his fingertips lightly to the skin beside the gauze and found it cool. He couldn't detect any sour aroma, either, so the cut likely wasn't infected. Whatever was bothering Luke, it wasn't his injury. "I'd like to thank you again for your help with Emilio last week," Jackson said. "The hospital staff told me his burns are healing well."

Luc closed his hand into a fist and smacked the bar, causing the coffee cup to rattle in its saucer. "Damn them."

"Who?"

"The Corbins. They're scum."

There had been no advantage to keeping the Marchands' suspicions about the Corbin brothers a secret—all the hotel employees had needed to be put on alert for their appearance and for any further attempts at sabotage. Because of that, Jackson didn't find Luc's statement unusual, but the vehemence with which he spoke seemed off. "We're doing everything we can," Jackson began.

"They have to be stopped before they hurt anyone else."

"We won't give them the chance."

"The Marchands have been good to me. They've treated me like family. They don't deserve this."

"No, they don't," Jackson said, pushing the cup closer to Luc. "They're good people."

Luc eyed the coffee. "I don't want that. I want another drink."

"It won't help."

"What?"

"Getting drunk. Avoiding a problem won't solve it. It'll still be there when you're sober, only it'll look even worse through a hangover."

Luc slumped forward, put his elbows on the bar and dropped his head into his hands.

Jackson looked past him to where Charlotte was sitting. She was still involved in her conversation with Melanie and Robert. Mac's men were circulating unobtrusively, keeping a watch on the patrons and the doorways. The singer started another number. Everything appeared normal, so Jackson returned his attention to Luc.

The man was deeply troubled. Jackson suspected it had to be about something more personal than the problems of his employer. "Is it money or a woman?" he asked.

Luc turned his head just enough to glare at Jackson through one eye. "What?"

"Whatever's bothering you."

Luc snorted. "Is this a hobby with you, going around sticking your nose into other people's problems?"

"As a matter of fact, it is," Jackson said. "I can't help it, been doing it all my life."

"Sure, it's easy to play the nice guy when you're born with a silver spoon in your mouth. You wouldn't understand what it's like to be on the outside looking in."

Jackson tilted his head. "I've never had money, Luc. I don't know where you got that idea."

"You're tight with the Marchand family. And you're a doctor."

Although Jackson might have been accepted by the Marchands, he doubted whether *Grand-mère* Celeste would ever change her opinion about him. But he wasn't going to start explaining that to Luc. "I'm a doctor because I won a full scholarship to Harvard," he said. "I couldn't have afforded even one year of state college on what I earned delivering refrigerators for my father's store. I know all about being on the outside looking in."

Luc's elbow slid against his coffee cup. He jerked upright and wiped the spatters from his sleeve. He was silent for a while, as if debating whether or not to go on. When he spoke again, his voice had lost its edginess. "My old man was born rich. Silver spoon, big mansion, the whole works, but his mother kicked him out."

"She must have had a reason."

A muscle twitched in Luc's jaw. "She did. He never saw that he brought it on himself. He blamed everyone else for trashing his life."

"Where is he now?"

"Dead."

Jackson watched him closely. He didn't believe Luc was drinking because of grief, so he didn't offer any condolences. Instead he waited in silence for the concierge to speak again.

Luc stared down at the coffee cup in front of him. "The problem is—" His voice hitched. He cleared his throat and grabbed the cup with both hands. "I blamed everyone but him, too. I never gave his family a chance. I thought I owed it to my old man to settle the score and now I've ended up trashing my own life."

"How, Luc?"

"It's too late to fix things."

It was hard to follow Luc's cryptic ramblings. Jackson took a stab anyway. "You want to reconcile with your family. That's what's bothering you, right?"

Luc moved his head back and forth in a slow negative. "There are too many lies. I don't know how."

"It's simple. Just tell them the truth."

Luc gulped down half the coffee, then coughed and wiped his eyes. He looked around the barroom, stopping when his gaze reached the table where Charlotte, Melanie and Robert sat. Abruptly he shoved himself off the stool.

Jackson grabbed his arm. "Careful there."

He jerked his arm free and staggered sideways a few steps. "You were right."

"Luc—"

"Sitting here getting drunk won't solve anything. That's the kind of thing my old man would have done." He smoothed his hair and straightened his tie, his hands shaking with the clumsy concentration of someone striving to appear sober. "I need to tell the truth."

Jackson frowned in concern. "Let Leo call you a taxi."

Luc patted his pockets and came up with a cell phone. "Thanks, doc, but I got it covered."

There was nothing more Jackson could do short of forcing the man back on the stool and waiting until he sobered up. Besides, his priority was to keep an eye on Charlotte, not to dispense free advice. He looked at her table, only to discover it was empty.

All thoughts of Luc were smothered by a surge of pure adrenaline. She was gone. God, *no!*

But the panic that kicked up his pulse was short-lived. Before he could get more than two strides from the bar, he heard her voice behind him.

"Hi, handsome. Do you come here often?"

He blew out his breath and pivoted to face her. She was smiling. A real smile, not one of her professional ones. The sight didn't exactly calm his pulse, but it brought it down to a rate reasonable. He tried to ignore the tightness that persisted in his chest—he didn't want to examine why he'd been so quick to panic in the first place.

Holding out his good hand, he endeavored to keep his voice casual. "No, I don't, but I heard this is where the most beautiful women are."

She took his hand and laced her fingers with his. The brief-case she'd brought into the bar with her was gone. Instead she held a white paper bag in her free hand. "Are you enjoying the music?"

"Sure. You were right—Holly's good. Did you finish your business?"

"Yes, we're all done. I made sure of it, see?" She held up the bag. "I traded my briefcase to Melanie for a midnight snack from Chez Remy."

"Sounds as if you got the better half of the deal. What's in there?"

She swung the bag behind her back. Her hair rippled as she shook her head. "Oh, no, you don't. It's not midnight yet."

He smiled at the note of teasing in her voice. This was more like the Charlie he used to know. He slid his arm around her waist, swaying gently to the beat of the music. "So what did you decide on for the ball? I'm guessing it wasn't po'boys and beer."

"Robert and Melanie want to pull out all the stops for this one. They said they intend to make it a night to remember."

"You're still not looking forward to it."

"I'm looking forward to it being over. The Corbins' offer expires at midnight, the same time we end the ball."

And once the hotel was no longer the target of a take-over, Jackson thought, his stay with Charlotte would be over, too.

But Yves would have finished the second test by then, anyway. If the news was good, he'd be scheduling surgery and Jackson could begin planning his return to work.

Charlotte laid her hand on his chest. "What's wrong?"

It was a good question. Why did the thought of getting what he wanted—of them both getting what they wanted—leave him feeling hollow?

The music slowed. The saxophone resonated with the

opening bars of an old torch song, a melody of loss and yearning. Jackson didn't want to listen to that—or to the questions in his head. He put his lips beside Charlotte's ear. "Want to go someplace where we can get naked?"

She laughed. "I thought you'd never ask."

ONLY A TRACE OF THE melody reached the courtyard, yet the longing in the notes came through loud and clear. Luc wove his way past the lounge chairs and moved into the shadow of a lemon tree. Leaning his back against the trunk, he inhaled deeply in an effort to clear his head.

It would be simpler to walk away and just keep going. He could talk himself into another job without any trouble, just as he'd talked himself into this one. People trusted him, they called him charming, and he'd always had the gift of making people like him. He'd inherited that talent from his father.

Just as he'd inherited his cowardice?

Luc regarded the cell phone he clutched in his hand. He didn't have to make the call. It still wasn't too late to cut his losses. If he left now, the Marchands would never have to know who he was. He could fade out of their lives the same way his father had. His grandmother hadn't mellowed—she was still the unbending tyrant who had banished her only son. He wouldn't miss her.

Yet he'd miss the others. Anne was a good woman, as were her daughters. They'd fought back against all the problems he'd caused during the past months and had kept the hotel going. They hadn't collapsed under pressure; they were the same generous, compassionate women he'd grown to know and admire. Their courage shamed him, as did their trust. He couldn't simply walk away and leave them to fend for themselves.

But the only way he could stay was by telling the truth. And if he did that, they might not want anything to do with him. Not that he could blame them...

He dropped his head back against the tree trunk. That was the point: he couldn't blame them. He shouldn't have in the first place. Too bad it had taken him so long to figure it out. As he'd told that doctor, he'd trashed his life. The best he could hope was that he'd end up in jail. That is, if Blount didn't have him killed first.

The thought sobered him faster than the fresh air. Luc glanced around the courtyard, but apart from a few groups of guests who strolled near the pool, he couldn't see anyone hanging around. That didn't guarantee anything, though. Mike Blount was planning something big, Luc was certain of it. The vandalism the Corbins had done was only a prelude. And no one was telling him anything, which didn't bode well. Every bit of common sense he possessed was warning him to get out now.

But his heart was telling him something else altogether. He'd believed the Marchands owed him, but it was the other way around. If he wanted the chance to be part of this family, he had to stop thinking about what he could take from them and start focusing on what he could give.

The music swelled to one last lingering note, then ended in a round of applause. Luc lifted his phone and dialed the number he'd found in Charlotte's office when he'd planted the Corbins' offer in her briefcase. He'd committed the phone number to memory days ago—some part of him had known all along that this was the only way out.

The voice that came on the line was businesslike yet still good-natured.

Luc took a steadying breath and began to speak. "Hello, Detective Fergusson, this is Luc Carter…."

CHAPTER TEN

CRÈME BRÛLÉE À LA Charlotte was one of four special desserts that Remy Marchand had created in honor of his daughters. The traditional elegant dish reflected the personality of his eldest. Made with eggs and rich, heavy cream, the custard needed skillful handling and slow cooking in order to achieve its full potential. The praline topping that completed it lent an air of polished grace, and at times it resisted being pierced, but once the shell was broken it quickly fell apart to reveal a lush, sensual center.

Normally the dessert was only available at Chez Remy, the hotel's four-star restaurant.

But Charlotte couldn't remember it ever tasting as good as it did here in her living room.

She parted her lips to let Jackson feed her another spoonful. The custard melted on her tongue instantly, sending a spurt of pleasure through the roof of her mouth. She curled her bare feet beneath her and leaned into the corner of the sofa. She was wearing nothing except Jackson's shirt, but it easily covered her thighs.

Jackson steadied the plate on the cushion between them and dipped his spoon back into the custard. "Your face is so expressive," he said, leaning forward to feed her another spoonful. "Just watching you eat that makes me feel as if I can taste it."

She licked a morsel from the corner of her mouth. "You probably can. You had most of it already."

"It was only the outside." He snatched a piece of the praline shell from the plate and popped it into his mouth. "And as everyone knows, sugar's energy food. I have to keep up my strength."

"Well, since you put it like that…" She took the spoon from his hand and scooped another piece for him. "Open up."

His eyes gleamed as he caught her hand. He let her feed him, then turned her hand so that he could lick the spoon. "Mmm."

Charlotte was amazed to feel a tiny aftershock of pleasure follow his hum of enjoyment. He'd made a similar sound a few minutes ago when they'd been in her bed. And as far as amazement went, it continued to astound her how readily she felt that pleasure at all. "I'll have to remember to thank Melanie."

Still holding her hand, he kissed each of her knuckles in turn. "Did she make the dessert?"

"No, desserts aren't her forte, but it was her idea to package it to go."

"I do like your sisters." He guided her hand back to the plate. "They come up with some excellent ideas."

"Oh?"

"Although next time ask Renee to give you a bigger box of condoms. At the rate we've been going through them, two dozen aren't going to be anywhere near—"

She stopped his words with another mouthful of custard.

He swallowed and lifted one eyebrow. "What?"

"You're getting a swelled head."

His lips twitched. "Charlotte, I'm not going to touch that one. It would be too easy."

She laughed and tossed the spoon onto the plate. "Oh, Jackson. This is *all* too easy."

"What is?"

"This." She waved her hand at herself and then at him. Although he'd put on his boxers when they'd gotten out of bed, he was completely comfortable with his near nudity. So was she. Sharing banter and a snack was comfortable, too. "I thought it would be harder," she said.

He winked. "Give me a few minutes and it will be."

"Oh, you're incorrigible."

"Incorrigible," he repeated. "I've been called worse." He moved the plate to the side table and patted his lap in invitation.

She slid across the sofa and snuggled into his embrace with a sigh. Although he couldn't grip her with his right hand, his arms held her as securely as she could have wanted. "This is nice."

He stroked a lock of hair from her cheek. "Does that mean I've redeemed myself?"

"Redeemed? What are you talking about?"

"I realize you haven't forgotten how bad I used to be at this."

Her brow furrowed. "If you're referring to those times when we were kids, they really don't matter."

"Don't they? I thought that's what you meant when you said this was easier than you'd expected."

"Jackson, I—"

"It's okay, Charlotte. My bumbling would have put anyone off. It's probably why you keep looking surprised."

"Surprised?"

He smoothed his index finger over her forehead, then rested

his hand on her hip. "Each time you climax, you get this look of shock. I guess you didn't believe I was capable of—"

"Jackson, you've got it wrong. I'm shocked at myself, not you."

"Why?"

She hesitated. Putting this into words made her seem almost pathetic, yet she didn't want Jackson to think she was judging him on his past performance. He'd been such a generous and considerate lover, she had to be honest. She placed her palm against his cheek. "Until yesterday, I'd never had an orgasm."

"You…" He blinked. "Never?"

She traced the line beside his mouth with her thumb. "I don't know why. I'm not a prude. I just never managed to achieve that particular goal."

His fingers tightened against her hip as he regarded her. Disbelief gradually gave way to a look of comprehension… followed by more than a hint of male smugness.

She didn't take issue with the smugness—he was entitled to it. "This isn't that big a deal, Jackson. I haven't dwelled on my lack and I've accepted who I am. My life has been full and very rewarding. Sex has never been important to me."

"You were married for eight years."

"Yes."

"And you never…?"

"No."

He moved his hand to her thigh and fingered the hem of the shirt she wore. "I had no idea."

"No one except my ex-husband does. For one thing, I was too embarrassed to discuss it. And for another, it wasn't relevant. I've been too busy with my work to think about romance, so I don't date. And now that I'm forty I'm quite settled with my life."

"But you're enjoying it now."

"Obviously. As you said, it has to be because of the circumstances." She tapped his chest. "And the chemistry between us."

"We've got lots of that." He leaned back against the arm of the sofa and stretched out one leg across the cushions, shifting her so that she was half lying on top of him. He stroked her hair for a while before he spoke again. "Is that why you divorced Adrian, Charlotte? Because you didn't have… chemistry?"

She should have known the topic wouldn't stay off-limits. She'd introduced it herself by talking about her sex life. "Not directly, but it was a contributing factor."

"How?"

"Adrian wasn't faithful, Jackson. I'm not sure when he started having affairs, but I didn't discover it until we'd been married almost five years."

"But you hung in for another three."

"I thought the fault was mine. I was so indifferent about our sex life, I couldn't really blame him for looking elsewhere, so I wanted to give him another chance. And on top of that, there was our business partnership."

Jackson's hand stilled. "Right. Your parents gave him a job."

"He was very valuable to the hotel."

"And the hotel's bottom line was more important to you than fidelity."

She heard the note of distance in his voice, yet she couldn't deny that what he'd said was true. What did it say about her if she'd willingly put up with a humiliating and unsatisfying marriage rather than risk hurting the family business?

But it hadn't only been the business she'd cared about, it had been her dream of a marriage like that of her parents, of sharing her life as well as her love.

"Yes," she said. "You could put it like that." She pushed herself off his chest and rose to her feet. "In the end, the hotel was more important to me than Adrian."

Jackson stayed where he was, sprawled across the sofa, but he no longer looked relaxed. This was a touchy subject for both of them. "Adrian Grant might have had blue blood and a pedigree, but he was a bastard anyway."

"Oh, more than you know." She rubbed her arms as she moved across the room. Jackson's scent rose from his shirt, making her feel as if he still held her. "Adrian knew how much I wanted children, Jackson. He claimed he wanted them, too, and that we would give them the same kind of unconditional love and deep roots that my parents had given my sisters and me. He insisted we take a house with a big yard and enough room for plenty of children, close to *Grand-mère* so they could visit every day. He spun a beautiful tale of the life I'd always wanted."

Jackson remained silent. She was grateful he did. It was the first time she'd spoken about this to anyone, and now that she'd started, she felt a need to finish. She paused beside the bookcase, her gaze falling on a photo of Daisy Rose. A lump formed in her throat as she thought of her niece's love for fairy tales. Maybe it would be kinder if Charlotte stopped reading them to her—believing in them only led to disappointment.

"When I failed to get pregnant," she said, "I thought it was because there was something wrong with me. Not medically—I went through all the tests—but I started to believe I wasn't enough of a woman so I wasn't meant to be a wife and mother. It wasn't until our eighth anniversary that I learned the truth. Adrian had had a vasectomy before we were married, only he had never bothered to tell me."

The sofa creaked. Jackson's bare feet made no noise on the carpet, but she could feel his approach. He spoke from over her shoulder. "Charlotte, I'm sorry."

"You said you never liked him. You always were a good judge of character."

"I didn't like him then because he was a snob. And because he married you." He rested his hand on her back. "I detest him even more now for the way he betrayed you."

"I should have seen it, Jackson, but I was so wrapped up in getting this make-believe future that I wanted, I couldn't see reality. Apparently Adrian had decided not to run the risk of fathering any illegitimate children during one of his affairs. That's why he'd had the vasectomy. He married me for prestige and for the chance to run the hotel, so he made an effort to be discreet. He didn't want to scandalize his family or hurt his image. He was always very conscious of his image. He spent more time in front of the mirror than I did, but that wasn't surprising since Adrian's first and only love was Adrian—" Her voice broke. She put her face in her hands. "*Mon Dieu*, how could I have been such a fool?"

Jackson took her by the shoulders and turned her toward him. "You weren't a fool, Charlotte. You were just going after your dream."

She dropped her hands and looked at Jackson.

It had been a mistake from the start to marry Adrian. She'd thought that she'd loved him, but how could she have? Their courtship had been a whirlwind. He'd been handsome and sophisticated, a veritable Prince Charming who happened to have a degree in hotel management. On the surface he had seemed like the perfect match for her. She hadn't taken the time to look deeper because she hadn't wanted to. She'd been on the rebound, desperate to fill the void in her heart that had formed when Jackson left.

With the type of unspoken understanding they used to share, Jackson widened his stance to slide his feet outside hers and drew her into his embrace.

Charlotte accepted his comfort gratefully, even as she strove to remind herself that this wouldn't last. Any feelings that she allowed to grow now would be as hopeless as they had been before.

So it was a very good thing she was being practical and realistic this time, and that they had both agreed that what was going on between them was only temporary and physical, right?

Right?

It had all seemed so clear when she'd woken up this morning, yet now...

She dropped her forehead into the hollow of his shoulder, just as she'd done countless times in the past. "I don't know if it's possible to love a thing the way you can love a person," she said. "But after my divorce, the hotel was all I had left of the life I had wanted. It's been my one constant. It's become more to me than just a business or a building, it's my framework and my anchor." Her voice dropped to a whisper as she slipped her arms around his waist. "Jackson, I honestly don't know what I would do without it."

JACKSON YANKED OPEN the front door with far more force than was necessary, causing it to smack into the stop that had been built into its frame. Wood creaked and hinges rattled, transferring the vibrations all the way up his arm. Charlotte gave him a quizzical look as she walked past him into the hotel.

He shrugged. "It slipped," he said, moving his hand to the small of her back.

She continued to regard him as they started across the lobby. "You've been in a strange mood this morning. Are you okay?"

"I'm fine." He forced a smile. "Where to first?"

"My office. I should catch up on my messages." She glanced past him. "That's odd. I wonder where Luc is."

Jackson turned his head and saw that the spot behind the concierge's desk where Luc usually stood was empty. "He's probably nursing a hangover," he commented.

"Luc? I didn't know he drank."

"He did yesterday. I saw him in the bar. He seemed upset about some problems he's having with his family."

"I know very little about Luc's family. He's been very private about his personal life—"

"Charlotte?"

At the sound of her name, Charlotte paused. Julie Sullivan, her assistant, was hurrying toward them from the front desk. She barely glanced at Jackson before she started into a list of problems. Charlotte went into what Jackson was beginning to think of as her manager's mode. This was how it had been every morning so far. The moment they walked through the door she became swallowed by the hotel.

And why not? As she'd told him the night before, it was her anchor. The one constant in her life. She loved it like a person.

The two women continued to discuss business as they headed for the grand staircase. Jackson shoved his hands into his jacket pockets and followed, making sure to stay close to Charlotte in spite of the milling guests. The place was more crowded today than he'd seen it yet. That was good. With Mardi Gras concluding in a little more than thirty-six hours, they needed this business if they wanted to stay solvent. He didn't want her to lose the hotel, did he?

No, of course not. She loved it. What kind of friend would he be if he wanted her business to fail? That was the whole idea behind staying with her—to make sure she wouldn't lose the one thing she loved.

I honestly don't know what I would do without it.

He waited as Charlotte unlocked her office door, then pushed it open and checked the room. There was no sign of disturbance. Everything was as it had appeared the previous evening. That was good, too. Right, everything was working out as well as either of them could have expected.

But somehow the door slipped from Jackson's grasp as he was closing it, slamming into the frame with enough force to shake the antique glass fanlight that was set into the wall above it.

Charlotte paused behind her desk, her suit jacket in her hand. She took her silver cell phone from the pocket and put it on the desk, draped the jacket neatly over the back of her chair and returned to where he stood. "Okay, what's going on?"

He flexed his fingers and looked at his hand. "I can't grip things that well. Sometimes it's hard to judge how much strength to apply."

She took his hand between both of hers and shook her head. "Don't try to snow me, Jackson. You've been on edge since we got up today. Waiting for Yves to rerun the nerve test tomorrow is getting to you, isn't it?"

She was right about that. The closer the test drew, the bigger it loomed. He clenched his jaw at the compassion in her voice. "I don't want your pity, Charlotte."

"I don't pity you. I thought you knew me better than that. My financial problems aren't the same as your physical one, but I do understand what you're going through." She lifted his hand to her face and pressed her cheek to his scarred palm. "Tomorrow's going to be a big day for both of us."

Once again he was struck by the irony of the situation. How had it happened that both of them were simultaneously facing the possibility of losing the very things they'd chosen to devote their lives to?

Yet he felt like a fraud for accepting her sympathy. Because as ugly as the thought was, deep inside he *did* want her to lose the hotel.

He'd claimed that he didn't hate this place, that he hadn't meant it when he'd told her he did, yet that wasn't the whole truth. There was a part of him that always would hate this hotel. Sure, it had been the backdrop for a large chunk of his growing-up years and there had been plenty of good memories for him in these walls, but the affection he felt for it had been tinged with envy. Charlotte had belonged here, but he never had.

And ultimately it had become his rival. That's why he hated it. Charlotte had chosen the hotel over him even before she'd married Adrian.

It still was his rival. In fact, she had moved into Jackson's arms, their bodies warm and pulsing from some of the best sex he'd ever had—and the best sex *she'd* ever had—and she'd stated flat out that she didn't know what she would do without the hotel.

You could come with me, he'd wanted to shout. If she lost the hotel, she would be free to leave with him.

But that wouldn't have occurred to her. Charlotte hadn't seen the alternative that was standing right in front of her nose.

Damn, he was surprised how that had hurt.

Yet it shouldn't have hurt. They'd both agreed that there were no strings to this affair, so he had no right to want more. They'd grown up, they knew the score, they didn't expect each other to change.

He eased away from her touch. "Sorry. You're right. I'm just stressed."

She chewed her lip briefly, then sighed. "I should apologize, Jackson."

"For what? I'm the one in the bad mood."

"It's because I talked about Adrian, isn't it? I noticed you got quiet after that."

He raked his fingers through his hair as he considered how to reply. This was water under the bridge. He'd worked through his anger about Adrian years ago, hadn't he?

Hell, no. He needed something else to slam. He walked to the window, braced his elbow on the side of the frame and glared at the wing of the building across the courtyard. "It would be smarter to leave this alone, Charlotte."

"I don't agree. If something's bothering you, let's talk about it. That's what you're always encouraging me to do."

"We've been getting along great. What good would it do to dredge up the past?"

Her heels tapped across the floor and stopped somewhere behind him. "Considering the foul mood you're in this morning, it probably would help to clear the air. That seems to have worked for us before."

"Are you sure you want me to be honest?"

"Always, Jackson."

He folded his good hand into a fist and smacked it against the window frame. "Fine. I appreciated your honesty when you told me about your marriage and I realize it was difficult for you to talk about it, but I'm not a saint, Charlotte." He turned to face her. "I tried to be understanding, but I can't forget that you dumped me for Adrian."

She reached out as if she were about to touch him but then pulled back her hand and crossed her arms. The sympathy in her gaze cooled to caution. "I didn't dump you, Jackson. You left me."

There it was, the past in a nutshell.

They'd danced around this issue for days without addressing it directly. They'd both done their best to ignore it. They'd kept things friendly, they'd spoken about the paths that they'd taken instead of the reasons behind them. But they had been waiting twenty years to finish this argument. Maybe it was high time they stopped waiting.

Some wounds needed to be lanced before they could heal.

"You did dump me, Charlie," he said. "We'd made plans. We promised we'd be together forever."

"Oh, I remember those plans, Jackson." Her voice hardened. "You changed everything when you accepted that scholarship."

"Nothing changed for me. I wanted you, not some old pile of bricks. Joining your family's business wasn't part of the package."

"It was as far as I was concerned."

"You made that clear. When I didn't fit into your vision of our future, you had no problem substituting Adrian."

"I was following my dream."

"And you sure were in a hurry to do it."

"Yes, I was." Color sprang to her cheeks as her words came faster. "That's what you were doing when you left me, wasn't it? Following your dream, no matter what it did to mine?"

"I asked you to come with me."

"And do what?"

Her shout hung in the air between them. That was the question that had stopped them before. She hadn't wanted to give up the hotel or her life here. "You wanted kids," he said. "We could have had kids."

"How? You were determined to leave for Africa as soon as you graduated. Did you expect me to uproot myself from my family, tag along with you like a piece of baggage and have our babies in a refugee camp? Or wait at home in some empty apartment for an absentee father whose children wouldn't even recognize him?"

He pinched the bridge of his nose, inhaling slowly to hang on to his temper. He wasn't sure whether he was angry with her or angry with himself for still feeling anything at all. "Do you remember that final Christmas? How I came home for the holidays?"

"Yes, I remember it vividly. That's when you told me you'd

committed yourself to working overseas and nothing I could say would change your mind."

"We hadn't seen each other for months. I wanted to make love, but you kept putting me off, saying you wanted to wait until our wedding night. I felt as if I was going to explode, but I respected your wishes. Less than two months later you married Adrian. Do you know what I thought?"

She stood by her desk and pressed her fingertips on the surface as if she needed to steady herself. "I explained it to you, Jackson. Our goals were incompatible."

"Sure, that's what you said. But I thought it was more. I thought he was better than me."

"What?"

"I believed Celeste was right, that you'd been slumming, that I was just a phase you had gone through. I thought that you had known all along you belonged with a man who had money and social graces and—"

"Jackson, no!"

"And I was convinced he had to be better in bed." He laughed humorlessly. "How's that for irony? I knew you hadn't liked sex with me. I figured Adrian must have been God's gift to women, a superstud, a sex machine. Thinking that he could give you what I couldn't drove me crazy."

"It wasn't like that."

"Sure. *Now* you tell me."

She sat on the edge of her desk. "Oh, Jackson. I'm so sorry. I had no idea...."

"Yeah, well, I got over it."

"Is that why you never married?"

"What?"

"Were you…concerned about—" She pressed her lips together.

"Was I concerned about my performance? Is that what you were going to ask?"

"I'm sorry. I have no right to probe."

He pushed away from the window and moved in front of her. He placed his hands on the desk beside her hips, caging her between his arms. "Do I strike you as a man who has problems in the bedroom?"

She shook her head.

"One of the benefits of being a doctor is a detailed knowledge of anatomy as well as an understanding of how a woman's body works." He leaned over her, bringing his face to hers. "I might have had a slow start, but I learned how to put that knowledge into practice."

"I noticed," she said tightly. "I asked you about marriage, not your sex life."

He dropped his gaze. She'd left the top button of her blouse open today. He could see her pulse flutter against the thin skin at the base of her throat. The scent that rose from her skin was a mixture of expensive perfume and the earthy honesty that had haunted him no matter how far he'd run.

And that was the true source of his anger. He knew damn well why he'd remained a bachelor. Losing the one woman he'd ever loved wasn't something a man forgot.

The pulse in Charlotte's throat accelerated.

Jackson stepped closer and nudged her knees apart with his leg. Nylon hose slid across the fabric of his pants, making a sound like a sigh. He'd watched her dress this morning. She didn't wear panty hose. Those stockings were held up by a garter belt of peach-colored silk. That was so like his Charlie, elegant and traditional on the outside but as sensual in her core as warm custard.

He hadn't realized he'd lowered his head until he felt her skin against his lips. He closed his eyes and kissed her throat, dipping his tongue into the hollow where he'd seen her pulse.

The phone that she'd placed on the desk began to ring. Charlotte put her hand on his chest.

"Let it go," he whispered.

She tilted her head away from him. "I can't."

He looped his arms behind her waist and slid her off the desk and into his body. The phone rang again. He straightened up, holding her off the floor so he could look into her face. "Charlie—"

"Put me down, Jackson. It could be important."

And this isn't?

Instead of releasing her, he flexed his arms, tightening his hold on her and flattening her breasts against his chest. At her gasp, he kissed her fast and deep, using his tongue to possess her as he wanted to use his body, fusing his mouth to hers while the phone continued to ring.

She grabbed his hair and yanked his head back. "Jackson, stop!"

Her grip wasn't gentle. The twinge of pain in his scalp helped bring him to his senses. So did the distress in her eyes. Jackson set her on her feet, held up his palms and stepped back.

Charlotte's hand shook as she wiped her mouth. "What was that supposed to prove?" she asked. Without waiting for his reply, she reached for the phone, spoke into it tersely, then carried it to the far side of the desk and turned her back on him.

Jackson wanted to kick something, but he doubted whether any of the furniture in this office would stand up to the force he would use. He returned to the window, threw it open and inhaled a lungful of fresh air.

What had he been trying to prove? That she would rather kiss him than do her job? That he could make her choose him over the hotel?

That the only tie between them was physical?

He already knew the answers to all those questions—and he didn't like any of them.

Staying with Charlotte had been a mistake. The smart thing to do would be to get out now, before things got worse. They were only going to end up hurting each other again.

A movement in the courtyard caught his eye. A man with sandy blond hair was staggering from the direction of the alley. It was Luc Carter, and he evidently was still drunk from the night before. He was bumping into guests, barely able to stay on his feet.

Jackson rubbed his face, still trying to clear his head, when Luc suddenly collapsed beside the pool.

For a split second Jackson didn't realize what he was seeing. Luc's blazer had fallen open, but instead of his typical white shirt, he was wearing red....

Luc wasn't drunk. He was soaked in blood.

CHAPTER ELEVEN

THE SMELL OF BLOOD wasn't something a person forgot. Not when there was this much of it. As Jackson knelt by Luc's side, decades of images kaleidoscoped through his head. He'd dealt with the aftermath of every kind of disaster, injuries caused both by nature and by man, so his response was automatic. Check the airway, assess the breathing and the circulation, tend to the basics first before searching for cause or treatment. Because treatment was moot if the patient didn't live long enough to receive it.

Yes, the professional in him functioned without hesitation. But he never got used to that quick spike of outrage he felt when he witnessed the damage that could be done to a human body. Luc was unconscious, his face sallow and his skin clammy. The volume of blood that soaked his shirt couldn't have been all that he'd lost. It was a wonder that he'd been able to walk anywhere under his own power.

Jackson glanced up only long enough to make eye contact with one of the people who had gathered around. It was a young man in a bright purple T-shirt, a half-eaten beignet gripped in his hand. "Bring me clean towels," Jackson said calmly. "As many as you can carry. There should be some stacked near the lounge chairs."

The young man dropped the pastry and bolted toward the pool. Beyond him, Jackson could see Mac jogging across the courtyard. He could hear Charlotte's voice from somewhere nearby as she spoke with the emergency operator. In spite of her high heels, she'd done her best to keep up with him as he'd raced outside. He was grateful now for her ever-present cell phone. But he didn't turn around to acknowledge her. He'd found the source of the blood: there was a small round hole in Luc's back.

Jackson had seen enough bullet wounds to recognize everything from the caliber to the angle of entry. This wound appeared to be from a .22, fired at close range. Not enough power to go clean through, but judging by the angle, it would have penetrated close to the liver. If that organ was nicked, Luc would be bleeding internally. This wound could prove fatal if he didn't get into surgery within the next half hour.

Even if Jackson had had the full use of both hands, without any medical equipment he wouldn't have been able to do more than apply pressure to the wound and keep the patient from going into shock. That was what he did now, improvising with the supplies that were available and directing several bystanders how to help. These first few minutes would be crucial to Luc's survival.

"The ambulance is on its way," Charlotte said. "So are the police. I also left a message for Detective Fergusson."

Jackson spoke without looking up. "The Corbins must be behind this."

"That was my first thought, too. But why would they want to hurt Luc?"

"Whatever their reason, they did a thorough job."

She touched his shoulder. "Is he going to make it?"

"It's impossible to say right now."

"I'm sure you're doing all you can. This is what you've been trained for."

He did look up then. She was standing beside him, her body stiff and her fingers white where she clutched her phone. Her cheeks were pale, but her lips were reddened and swollen from the force of his kiss.

Guilt tightened his stomach. How could he begin to explain his behavior, let alone apologize for it? He never would have forced himself on her, but he shouldn't have used the kiss as an outlet for his frustration. "Charlotte…"

She wouldn't meet his gaze. "Oh, Mac," she said, looking past Jackson. "Would you please have your people clear a path for the ambulance? And Julie, could you guide our guests indoors, please? I'm sure they'd be more comfortable there."

Jackson turned back to his patient. This wasn't the time to sort things out with Charlotte. And what was there to sort out? All he'd succeeded in doing was confirm that nothing had changed.

By the time the ambulance arrived, several uniformed police officers were already busy inspecting the scene and getting statements from the onlookers who were still in the courtyard. The paramedics who took over from Jackson were a different pair from the ones who had worked here the night of the fire, but they functioned with the same practiced efficiency. As they stabilized Luc for the trip to the hospital, Jackson helped himself to a bottle of sanitizer from their supplies and began to clean the blood from his hands.

"He's coming around," one of the paramedics said.

Jackson hurried to the stretcher. He was surprised that Luc

was rallying, considering the graveness of his condition. Yet when Jackson reached his side, Luc's eyes were open.

"Take it easy, Mr. Carter," the paramedic said. He hooked the end of the stretcher on the back of the ambulance and reached for the lever that would fold up the wheels. "You're going to be fine."

Luc thrashed his head back and forth. His lips parted, but it was impossible to hear what he was trying to say.

Jackson patted his shoulder above the restraint that strapped him to the stretcher. "Luc, it's Jackson Bailey. You've been shot. Don't try to move around or you could make your injury worse."

Luc rolled his head toward Jackson's voice. "Stop. Gotta stop…them."

"Who, Luc?"

"Corbins. Blount." His chest heaved with his efforts to breathe. "Fergusson."

"Did the Corbins do this to you, Luc?"

"Fergusson," he repeated.

"He's on his way. I'll tell him what you said."

"Stop!" Luc stared blankly at Jackson. "Charlotte. They're—" His words ended in a cough.

"Excuse me, Doctor," the paramedic said. He slid the stretcher past Jackson into the ambulance. "You'll have to step back now."

Jackson disregarded him and climbed into the vehicle with Luc. "What about Charlotte?" he demanded, leaning over the stretcher.

Luc panted shallowly, obviously near the end of his strength. "They're going…take her."

"Take her? What do you mean?"

"Heard them. They thought—" He coughed again, more weakly than before, yet he appeared determined to speak, whatever the cost. "Thought I was dead... They said...get hotel...kidnap...Char—" Luc's eyes rolled back. His movements ceased.

Jackson pressed his fingertips below Luc's ear, automatically searching for a pulse. It was weak but still there.

And that was as far as his medical efforts went. Without another thought for his patient, Jackson jumped out of the ambulance and scanned the courtyard.

Charlotte was no longer in sight.

When had she left? He hadn't noticed. He'd been so focused on doing his job that he hadn't seen her go. He borrowed a cell phone from the paramedic and punched in Charlotte's number, but his call was routed to her voice mail. Jackson tossed the phone back to the paramedic and told him to relate what they'd heard to the cops, then ran toward the entrance to the bar, where Mac stood. "Have you seen Charlotte?" he called.

"She was here a minute ago," Mac replied. "She said she was going inside to check Luc's personnel file for his next of kin."

Jackson grasped Mac's arm hard. "Notify your people. Tell them to find Charlotte and stick with her. Luc said the Corbins plan to kidnap her."

Mac didn't waste time with questions. He had his phone to his ear and was already giving orders before Jackson turned away.

Jackson glanced at the open window of Charlotte's office as he ran across the courtyard toward the lobby entrance. If she'd wanted to check Luc's personnel file, she must have gone upstairs. But why wasn't she answering her phone? He should have kept better track of her. That's why he was here— to protect her, to watch over her, to ensure her safety.

The single whoop of a siren echoed briefly from the hotel walls. He didn't pause to watch the ambulance drive away. That could have been why Luc had been shot, to provide a distraction. With everyone's attention focused on Luc, anyone could have walked into the hotel.

Charlotte wasn't in the lobby, but a small silver cell phone that looked like hers was lying on the floor at the base of the staircase.

Jackson snatched it from the floor. Yes, it was Charlotte's. He'd seldom seen her without it. She wouldn't have dropped it accidentally....

The adrenaline surge Jackson had felt the night before, when he hadn't seen Charlotte in the bar, had been merely a foretaste of what he felt now. Trying to think rationally didn't work. The sense of emptiness that spread through his body was turning his blood to ice.

He'd known he was going to lose her again but not so soon. God, not like this.

Jackson glanced up at the curving staircase, then reversed direction and sprinted to the street. He was going on instinct rather than logic. From the corner of his vision he could see two of the hotel's security guards moving purposefully toward the corridor that led to the art gallery and the event rooms, but he didn't pause. He burst through the front entrance. "Charlie!"

A long black limo was idling down the street from the hotel, its wheels encroaching on the sidewalk. A large man in a chauffeur's cap was closing the rear door when a woman's high-heeled shoe tumbled from the opening.

Jackson dived for the car and grabbed the edge of the door, trying to force it open. "Charlie!"

He only had a moment to glimpse the scene inside the limo, yet the image became seared into his brain. Charlotte was on the floor of the car, her legs a blur of motion as she fought to kick out at the men who held her. Dan Corbin had his arm locked around her throat and his other hand flattened across Charlotte's mouth. Richard jammed a black revolver into the side of her ribs.

But that was all Jackson saw. An instant later, pain exploded through his skull. He was out cold before his face hit the pavement.

CHARLOTTE DIDN'T WANT to cry. She couldn't permit herself the luxury of falling apart, even in private. She had to be practical. The Corbins could return at any time. She should be formulating a plan of escape.

But even if the door to this room swung open and a clear route to freedom appeared, she wouldn't leave. Not without Jackson.

She cradled his head on her lap and peered at his face. There were no windows in this place. The only light came from a bare bulb in the center of the ceiling. It was more like a closet than a room, less than six feet wide and scarcely ten feet long. There were rows of holes in the cement-block walls, as if there had once been shelves fastened there, but nothing was stored in here now. All that was left on the musty cement floor were some flattened pieces of cardboard.

Charlotte shivered. Her silk blouse and short skirt provided little protection against the damp air, and her legs were going numb from kneeling on the cardboard, yet she didn't want to move around. She didn't want to leave Jackson. "Wake up," she whispered. "Please, Jackson, open your eyes."

There were purple bruises on Jackson's forehead and right cheek and a lump on the back of his skull, but there had been no bleeding, thank God. The dried blood that smeared his cuffs and the front of his jacket wasn't his, it was Luc's. She tried to reassure herself that Jackson was going to be all right, that he was only temporarily knocked out, but her hope wasn't based on any medical expertise. No, there was nothing logical about her feelings, she simply couldn't imagine losing him.

It was because of her that he was hurt.

Yet this wasn't the first time he'd been hurt because of her, was it?

She blinked hard, trying to keep the tears from falling, but one rolled down her cheek and dropped on Jackson's forehead. She wiped it away, then ran her fingertips into his hair and automatically smoothed it back.

Their survival was at stake. This wasn't the time to dwell on that horrible scene in her office. They were facing far more important issues than their personal relationship.

But it was as impossible to shut out the echoes of his anger as it was to shut off her fear.

All these years she'd resented Jackson for deserting her, but he'd had plenty of cause for resentment himself. She should have realized how sensitive he would have been about the difference between his background and Adrian's, yet it had been such a nonissue for her she hadn't dreamed he would have considered it.

And she'd held herself responsible for their failure at sex—she'd never guessed he would have blamed himself.

She licked at a tear that trickled into the corner of her mouth, passing her tongue over the welt on her lip. Most of the swelling was from Dan Corbin's rough treatment. But not all. Some of the tenderness was from having her lip crushed against her teeth by Jackson's kiss.

How was it that two people who cared so much about each other seemed destined to keep inflicting more pain on each other?

Men's voices sounded from somewhere in the corridor beyond the room. Charlotte looked at the flat steel door, her pulse tripping with dread. She recognized Richard Corbin's cigarette-roughened drawl and the calmer tones of his brother, but there was a third voice that was unfamiliar. Could it belong to the chauffeur who had struck Jackson? Although she strained to listen, the conversation was too far away for her to make out the words. Moments later it faded completely.

Jackson's breathing changed, growing more rapid. A groan rumbled from his throat.

Charlotte stroked his cheek. "Jackson?" she murmured. "Can you hear me?"

He moved his head against her thighs. "Charlotte? What…?"

"You were hit on the head." She placed her hand near the spot behind his ear where she'd found the bump. "Are you okay? Is there anything I can do?"

He opened his eyes. His gaze was unfocused, wandering around the room as if he didn't register what he was seeing, before it finally steadied on hers. He touched the back of his fingers to her neck. His hand was shaking. "Did they hurt you, Charlotte?"

Her lip throbbed, her throat ached from Dan's choke hold and her side was bruised from where Richard had shoved his gun, but those discomforts were minor. She had no cause to complain.

Except that Jackson was calling her Charlotte. He'd called her Charlie when he'd kissed her and when he'd tried to stop the Corbins. Now he'd gone back to Charlotte. Somehow it made the ache in her throat worse.

"I'm fine," she said.

He rolled away from her lap and sat up quickly, then clenched his jaw and pressed the heel of his hand against his head.

"Oh, be careful," Charlotte said. "They hit you awfully hard."

Jackson breathed slowly through his nose for a while before he shifted to his knees. "I tried to stop them, but I didn't do much good."

"Don't blame yourself, Jackson. It's my fault. I should have been more careful, but I was worried about Luc and wasn't paying attention to my surroundings. The Corbins came out of nowhere."

"They were counting on Luc to be a distraction."

"Is he…?"

"Luc's a fighter. The last I saw of him, he was still hanging on." He patted his pockets. "Damn, they took the phone."

"You had a phone?"

"I found yours in the lobby." He looked around. "Where are we?"

"I don't know. After they knocked you out, they blindfolded me and—" Her breath hitched as she remembered the terror of that ride. "I couldn't see you. I didn't know how badly you were hurt until they dumped us in here. Are you sure you're okay?"

He ran his fingers along the back of his head, then scrutinized them. "No blood, not much swelling. I've probably got a mild concussion, that's all. I'll have a headache for a while, but it won't need treatment." He peeled off his jacket and reached out to swing it around her shoulders.

She started to shrug it off. "No, Jackson, you need this."

"You're shivering."

"I'm all right."

"Now's not the time to be stubborn, Charlotte," he said. "Keep the jacket. I can hear your teeth chattering."

She slid her arms into the sleeves and his warmth enveloped her instantly. So did his scent, chasing away the dank smell of the room. She rolled the cuffs back above her wrists, remembering that she'd worn Jackson's shirt the night before. It seemed impossibly long ago now.

"Better?"

She swallowed against another wave of tears. "Everything's such a mess. How did we end up like this?"

He regarded her in silence, as if he wasn't sure whether she was referring to what was happening to them or what was happening between them.

He chose the less personal topic. "Luc overheard the Corbins plan to kidnap you. They obviously intend to hold you until Anne signs the hotel over to them."

"She won't do that."

"She'll do it in a heartbeat."

Charlotte overlapped the front edges of Jackson's jacket and crossed her arms over the extra folds of denim. Paper crackled in the breast pocket. Dimly she remembered that Marie had slipped the package with her gris-gris in there. God, that seemed impossibly long ago, too. "Mama can't give up," she murmured. "It's more than just a pile of old bricks to her. She knows how important—"

"Anne loves you. She would never choose the hotel over you."

Somehow the topic was turning personal anyway. Charlotte inhaled shakily and pressed her back against the wall. "I'm sorry, Jackson."

"I'm sorry, too." He braced his knuckles on the floor and shoved himself upright. He swayed for an instant, bumping into the wall with his shoulder, until he stretched out his arm to steady himself. He walked to the door and tried the latch. It didn't move. "I should have been thinking of you, but I was too wrapped up in my job."

"I didn't mean I'm sorry about this situation," she said, waving her hand at the room. "Although I am. But I was talking about what happened…before."

He studied the door for a while, then returned to stand in front of her. He squatted and rested his forearms on his thighs. "So was I, Charlotte."

The light from the bare bulb overhead was harsh. It accentuated the bruises on Jackson's face and the taut lines beside his mouth. It also made the sadness in his eyes impossible to miss.

She wiped her cheeks, not surprised to find them wet. "I never cry, you know. I don't lose my temper or raise my voice either. But since you came home, I can't seem to stop doing all three."

"The hotel was your home, not mine," he said. "I was always a visitor."

They were picking up the argument where they'd left off, except the passion was gone. That made it even sadder. Charlotte dropped her head back against the wall. "We've been abducted and locked into a windowless closet by a pair of criminals who are bent on stealing my family's legacy. Doesn't it strike you as strange that we're still pulling apart our past?"

"Maybe. But now that we've opened the wound, we might as well let it drain."

"Always the doctor."

"Exactly. I'll always be a doctor. It's who I am."

"I know. I've seen you in action. It's what you were meant to do."

His jaw tightened as he regarded his hands. The harsh light made the scar on the right one appear darker and longer than usual. "That's true now, but it started out as a way to prove myself. That's why I went into medicine instead of taking over my father's appliance business or joining you at the hotel. I needed to feel I was worth something."

"Jackson—"

"You said earlier that you wanted me to be honest. You deserve to hear all of it."

She hugged his jacket more tightly as she looked around their prison. Maybe it wasn't so strange that they were continuing the discussion. Jackson would have realized as well as she did that if they didn't finish this now, they might not get another chance.

"I saw medicine as a means to give value to my life," he said. "It was one way to put my meddling nature to good use. But that wasn't the main reason I was so eager to accept that scholarship. I saw it as an opportunity to get out of New Orleans."

"What?"

"You had a big family and deep roots, along with money and a snazzy hotel. I was jealous of it all. I felt I couldn't compete. I knew that I'd never be happy here. Even as we were making all those plans when we were in high school I realized they weren't for me. Once I left, I never intended to come back."

Her throat closed. He really *had* meant to leave her. Hearing him admit it stirred all the old pain.

"My motives weren't noble," he continued, "they were selfish. I thought if I left, I could force you to give up your life here and choose me." He briefly touched his index finger to her swollen lip. "I was wrong to try to force you. I'm sorry, Charlotte."

She nodded.

He withdrew his hand, backed up and sat on the floor across from her. "That's the real reason working overseas first appealed to me," he said. "I wasn't thinking about what would make you happy, I was mainly concerned with myself."

The same could be said about her, she thought. She hadn't considered what would have made Jackson happy when she'd stubbornly refused to go with him. Her dreams of a fairy-tale future had been centered around the needs of the princess, not the prince. "I stayed behind because I wanted you to prove your feelings by choosing me over your career."

"I know."

"It wasn't right."

"Neither of us was right."

She licked away another tear. The problems between them

had gone deeper than she'd imagined. "We really did make a mess of things."

"Yeah." He pulled up his legs and propped his arms on his bent knees. "But even if we could rewrite the past, it wouldn't make any difference because no matter what detail we changed, we'd still be the same people."

How often in the last few days had she told herself the same thing? As much as they tried not to, perhaps they really were destined keep hurting each other.

Yet her dream for her future hadn't been only about the hotel or children or working as a partner with her husband. At its core, her dream had been about love, but she'd been too stubborn to make that her priority.

She should have. She'd loved Jackson from the first moment she'd seen him, the gangly boy with the crazy hair, the crooked smile and a gaze the color of a summer sky.

She loved the man he'd become even more.

The realization was no surprise. It was as undeniable as the tears that continued to trail down her cheeks. Oh, yes. She loved him. She'd never stopped. Why else was she crying? She'd done her best to rationalize it away, to call it nostalgia or stress or sex, but there was no mistaking what was in her heart.

She was in love with Jackson Bailey.

Again.

Still.

Probably forever.

And she had this grand realization when they were trapped in a windowless closet, at the mercy of criminals who were fully capable of killing them.

"Jackson?"

The look he gave her was hard to interpret. His eyes held regret mixed with the sadness, and his jaw was set with what could have been pain.

The words she wanted to say died in her throat. What good would a confession do now? It might make her feel better, but it would make Jackson feel worse. He hadn't wanted this complication. He'd been adamant about that from the start. She should be thinking of his needs, not hers. She shifted to her knees and crawled across the space between them. Without any preamble, she placed her hands on either side of his face and kissed him.

He responded gently, barely moving his lips, as if he worried about hurting her again.

She sobbed and opened her mouth, giving vent to her frustration. With the understanding he'd always shown, he slid his hand into her hair to hold her steady and deepened the kiss.

For a few precious minutes the floor didn't seem as hard or as cold and the fear that sat on her shoulder was shrugged aside. She was once more his Charlie, in love with her Jackson, and life had limitless possibilities.

And oh, *God,* she wished with all her heart that she still believed in magic.

There was a sudden clunk from the other side of the room's steel door.

Jackson got to his feet. Charlotte scrambled to stand beside him, but he caught her arm and guided her behind his back just as the door swung open.

Richard Corbin stepped into the doorway. He was holding a small black gun, probably the same one he'd used to force

Charlotte into the car. Had he also used it to shoot Luc? Pointing the gun at Jackson, he stepped to the right of the door frame and pressed his back to the far wall so that he maintained the maximum distance between them. "It's about time you woke up. You were one heavy bastard to drag."

Jackson spread his feet apart and crossed his arms. "What do you want, Corbin?"

"You're not that stupid. You know what we want. The Hotel Marchand."

Charlotte moved to Jackson's side. She'd lost her shoes somewhere between here and the hotel and she missed the illusion of confidence the extra few inches in height would have given her. Still, she wasn't going to let this criminal see her cower. She drew herself up to her full five feet three inches and fixed Richard with a cold stare. "This is an outrage, Mr. Corbin. I demand that you release us immediately."

He swung the barrel of the gun toward her. "Not before we get what we've come for."

Jackson placed himself in front of Charlotte again. "If you think you can get the hotel through means like these, you're mistaken."

"Wrong." He gestured with his gun. "And you can skip the human-shield heroics, doc. We don't plan to kill her yet."

Yet? Oh, God, Charlotte thought. This couldn't be happening.

As if he could feel her horror, Jackson moved his arm behind his back and held his hand palm up in invitation. Charlotte clasped it gratefully, lacing her fingers with his.

"It's not too late to get yourself out of this, Richard," Jackson said. "Luc isn't dead. You're not facing a murder charge."

Richard laughed. "Luc? Wrong again. He's dead, all right. I heard he never made it to the hospital."

Charlotte pressed closer to Jackson's back, fighting to keep her whimper inside. She didn't want to believe that the charming young man her family was so fond of could have succumbed to his wound. It seemed so unreal. Was that going to be her and Jackson's fate?

Dan Corbin moved over the threshold and joined his brother at the side of the doorway. While Richard appeared edgy, his older brother was unruffled, his tie straight and his hair neatly brushed. He looked as calm as if he were conducting a normal business meeting.

Charlotte's sense of unreality deepened. How could either of these men think they could get away with criminal behavior like this?

Dan looked at Charlotte. Instead of a gun, he held a roll of duct tape in his hands. "Come here," he ordered.

Jackson squeezed her fingers to keep her where she was. "The Marchands aren't going to sell, Dan. You'd be better off releasing us now—"

Richard pointed his gun toward the wall and fired.

Charlotte screamed and clapped her hands over her ears. The bullet burrowed harmlessly into the wall amid a puff of dust and crumbled brick, but the noise of the shot in the small room was deafening.

"The next one's for your boyfriend," Richard shouted. "Now get over here."

Charlotte lowered her hands. "Don't hurt him."

"Then do what we tell you."

She tried to slip past Jackson, but he barred her way with

his arm. "She's not going anywhere without me, Richard," he said. "And unless you're a damn good shot, that .22 you're holding isn't powerful enough to stop me from reaching you before you can pull the trigger a second time."

"If you try anything, I'll shoot her," Richard said.

Jackson's reply was eerily calm. "If you hurt her, I will kill you."

Dan ripped off a piece of duct tape. "We're wasting time," he said. "We'll bring them both."

CHAPTER TWELVE

MIKE BLOUNT LIFTED THE wineglass to his nose and inhaled greedily. It was the good stuff, more than two hundred bucks a bottle retail, so he was going to enjoy every ounce of it. This was a night for celebration. The next time he cracked open one of these bottles, he'd be doing it from his own private table in that fancy restaurant at the Hotel Marchand. Crystal and white linen. Only the best from now on.

He took a sip and held it in his mouth, savoring the taste. Then he placed the glass on his desk, checked his watch and pointed to the phone. "It's time, Dan."

For once, Dan Corbin didn't hesitate to obey the order. He picked up the phone and dialed.

Mike smiled and leaned back in his chair. The Corbin brothers weren't good at thinking for themselves. They'd had the right idea last week when Richard had tried to abduct Anne—the threat of death was always a good motivater when it came to getting people to fall into line—but they'd chosen the wrong Marchand.

Mike slid his gaze to the woman in the corner of his office. The eldest of the Marchand daughters was the general manager of the hotel. It was mainly because of her that the Corbins' plan to ruin the business had failed to produce the desired results. She was the most dedicated of the four sisters, she lived and breathed for that hotel, so even if her mother didn't agree to sell now, the place wouldn't survive long without Charlotte.

Either way, Mike was going to get what he wanted.

"Hello, Mrs. Marchand," Dan said. "Have you signed the contract?"

Until now Charlotte had been keeping her expression blank. She had refused to meet Mike's gaze, angling her chin in the air as if she were sitting at some tea party and he was the hired help. He didn't know how she pulled it off—in that oversize, stained denim jacket, dusty skirt and torn hose, she should have appeared ridiculous. Yet even with a few yards of duct tape wrapped around her torso to hold her to the metal chair where she sat and more duct tape binding her wrists and covering her mouth, she still managed to look down her nose at him.

As soon as she realized that her mother was on the other end of that phone, though, those elegant green eyes of hers filled with panic.

"Yes, she's alive," Dan said.

Mike gestured to Richard, enjoying himself more than he had thought possible. "Remove the tape from her mouth," he said. "Let her say hello to her mama."

Richard's gaze flicked uneasily to the man who was bound to the chair beside Charlotte.

His hesitation was understandable. Although Mike didn't doubt the information Otis had given him was accurate, Jackson Bailey didn't act like any doctor that Mike had met before. Despite the duct tape that held him motionless and the gun Richard kept trained on him, he looked like a dangerous man. It wasn't because of his physique, although with his height and his solid build he could do some serious damage if he got loose. No, it was his eyes.

This man understood the situation. He appeared to miss nothing as he studied his surroundings and his captors. He had the look of someone who had seen death often enough to recognize it. Unlike the hothouse-flower Marchand woman, he appeared to realize that Mike couldn't afford to let either of them leave here alive.

Mike snapped his fingers. "Richard!"

Keeping his gun trained on the doctor, Richard sidled up to Charlotte's chair, gripped one edge of the duct tape that covered her mouth and gave it a swift yank.

Tears brimmed in her eyes, but she didn't make a sound. It was the doctor who flinched. He looked at her, then fixed Richard with a stare that made him take a reflexive step backward.

Mike tried to contain his impatience. "Remove her boyfriend's gag, too," he ordered.

Richard pressed the muzzle of his gun against Charlotte's neck, reached across her and ripped away the tape that covered Jackson's mouth. Once he'd accomplished that, he backed away with a bravado that was close to recklessness.

The Corbins had nearly fulfilled their purpose, Mike reminded himself. Until this point they had been his go-betweens, doing his dirty work so that his hands remained clean. He wouldn't have to put up with them much longer. "Dan?" he prompted.

Dan carried the phone to Charlotte and pressed the receiver to her ear. "Go ahead."

Charlotte spoke immediately. "Mama, I'm all right. So is Jackson. Please don't worry. We—"

"That's enough," Dan said, pulling the phone away. "As you heard, Mrs. Marchand, your daughter is alive. How long she stays that way is up to you. Now I'm asking you again, have you signed the contract?"

There was a pause. Dan lowered the phone and looked at Mike. "She wants to know why your name's on this one instead of ours."

Mike snapped his fingers again and held out his hand for the phone. He was going to enjoy this, too. "Hello, Mrs. Marchand," he said. "This is Mike Blount."

"Who are you?" The voice that came through the phone was as sweet as warmed honey in spite of the anxiety in the words. It took generations of good breeding to produce a classy accent like that, along with a lifetime of wealth. Anne Marchand sounded exactly as Mike had thought she would— he would bet if he could see her, she would be looking down her nose at him, just as her daughter was.

"I'm a business associate of the Corbins, Mrs. Marchand," he said.

"Please don't let them hurt my daughter."

"I'll do my best, but the Corbins are desperate men. They're in financial difficulty, just like you. Simply put, they are in my debt, and to pay me back they have promised to acquire your property for me." He smiled as he looked at Charlotte. "We do have a deal, don't we, Mrs. Marchand?"

"Yes, yes!" Anne cried. "Let Charlotte and Jackson go."

"And the contract?"

"It's signed and notarized, exactly as Dan Corbin asked."

"Excellent. Place it at the concierge's desk in the main lobby. Someone will be there shortly to pick it up. And no cops," he added, "or the deal is off."

"I haven't told anyone, I swear."

Mike's warning had only been for show. He knew that Anne hadn't called the police. According to Otis, the Marchand women hadn't said anything about the kidnapping, in spite of his questions. They'd maintained complete silence as soon as they had received the ransom demand. There was no buzz around the station or through any of Otis's contacts either. Everyone at the hotel had closed ranks—they were following Mike's demands to the letter.

"What about my daughter and Jackson?" Anne asked.

"As soon as I receive the contract, they will be released."

"How? Where?"

"We'll be in touch," Mike said. "Oh, and one last thing, Mrs. Marchand."

"Yes?"

"I expect your cooperation to continue. Otherwise…" He paused to let the threat sink in. "You have three other daughters. You have a granddaughter, as well. A lively child, from what I've heard."

"What—" Her voice cracked. "What do you mean?"

"If you attempt to void this contract by claiming it was signed under duress or if you speak to the police now or at any point in the future, someone else in your family will suffer the same fate as your eldest daughter."

"*Mon Dieu.*" Anne's voice was no more than a whisper. "You can have the hotel. I won't say anything. Please, I beg you, just leave my family alone."

Mike terminated the connection and placed the phone on his desk. He savored the moment for a while—the taste of victory was almost as good as the wine.

"Did she go for it?" Dan asked.

Mike nodded once. "Yes. The Hotel Marchand is mine."

Richard pumped his fist in the air and reached for the wine bottle. "This calls for a toast."

"Put that down," Mike ordered. "We're not finished yet. I need you to go outside and wait for my driver."

Richard glanced at Dan. There was an almost imperceptible nod again.

Mike slapped his palm on the desk, making both Corbins jump. "Outside, both of you. And leave the gun beside the bottle, Richard. I might need it."

After a telling hesitation, Richard laid his gun on the desk. Dan straightened the knot of his tie and cleared his throat. "So we're square now, right, Mike?"

"Certainly, Dan. I'm a man of my word. Once my driver gets here with the purchase contract, we can consider your debt to me paid in full."

Mike listened to their footsteps ring on the steel staircase outside his office, then watched through the glass wall until they had crossed the warehouse floor. The Corbins were going to meet more than simply his driver, they were going to meet their fate. He glanced at the gun and smiled. How obliging of Richard to leave a clear set of fingerprints. Apart from the necessity of having Carter killed sooner than Mike would have preferred, this was all working out exactly as he'd planned.

"You'll get what you asked for," Jackson said. "Let us go."

Mike took his time topping up his wineglass before he replied. "I believe you understand why I can't do that."

Jackson looked at Charlotte, then back at Mike. "I understand you need to demonstrate your power to the Marchands to leave them too terrorized to back out of the deal. You can accomplish that by killing me instead of Charlotte."

After having to endure the Corbins, it was refreshing to speak with an intelligent man for a change. Mike could see that the doctor wasn't like the Marchands, either. He was educated, but his speech didn't have the polish of old class. The guy had guts, too.

Charlotte twisted her head to look at Jackson. "What are you doing?"

Jackson kept his gaze on Mike. "Surgeons are well paid. I donate the bulk of my income to charity, but my fees from last year are still in my bank. You can have it all as long as you let Charlotte go."

It was tempting to take him up on the offer. Mike seldom turned down an easy profit, and one dead body could be as much a deterrent as two. "This is a first for me," he mused. "I don't believe I've ever had a man offer me money to execute him rather than someone else."

Charlotte's chair wobbled as she strained against the tape that held her. "Jackson, no!"

"Stay out of this, Charlotte."

"I won't leave here without you."

"Yes, you will. And you're going to swear that you won't go to the police."

"No, it's me they wanted in the first place, not you." She looked at Mike. "Let Jackson go. You don't need him anymore."

Mike took what he calculated was a twenty-dollar mouthful of wine and swished it through his teeth. She wasn't looking down her nose at him now, he thought. If he asked her to, she would probably get down on her knees. Chuckling, he leaned over to open the top drawer of his desk and drew out one of the skinning knives that Otis had returned to him. "This is all very touching, but business is business." He stroked the flat of the blade with his thumb. "I've waited a long time to get my hands on the Hotel Marchand. And believe me, I didn't get where I am today by leaving any loose ends."

JACKSON FOUGHT TO KEEP his expression impassive as he worked at his own loose end. The edge of the duct tape wasn't flat. Dan had been in too much of a hurry to smooth it out when he'd bound Jackson's wrists, and as a result, there was a corner that hadn't adhered fully. After more than thirty minutes of painstaking effort, he had finally succeeded in pushing his right index finger beneath the gap.

It wasn't much—the tape was looped around his wrists three times and would have to be unwound millimeter by millimeter if Jackson was going to free himself—but at this stage he was willing to grasp at the smallest straw of hope… even if he was unable to grasp.

He wasn't sure how much time they had left, but he prayed it would be enough to break free. It felt as if he were touching the tape through a wall of glass shards. The ache that had been building in his strained tendons was getting worse. Muscles that hadn't responded in weeks were screaming in protest. He could almost feel the tissue that had managed to heal ripping apart, cell by cell.

Damn, he wished he had two good hands. Not so he could be a surgeon. No, he couldn't care less whether he ever held another scalpel or tied another bandage. He wanted his nerves to mend so that he could save one life, not hundreds.

"I'm sorry, Jackson."

The whisper was so faint he wasn't sure that he'd heard it. He turned his head and saw that Charlotte was looking at him, her eyes blurred with tears.

There were so many things they both could apologize for, it made no difference what she meant. He shook his head quickly—he didn't want her to waste the time they had left with regrets—but the motion made the ache from his concussion worse. He gritted his teeth to bring the pain down to a manageable level.

"This is all because of the hotel, and you never wanted any part of it," she whispered. "I'm so sorry you got dragged into—"

"Stall," he whispered.

"What?"

Jackson flicked his gaze behind his chair meaningfully. "Get Blount talking again. Keep him distracted."

Charlotte glanced at where Jackson's wrists were bound behind his back.

"What are you two whispering about?" Blount demanded.

"I remember you now, Mr. Blount," Charlotte said.

Jackson resumed his efforts to unwind the tape. Although Charlotte's face was tight with tension, she had gone into her tea-in-the-parlor mode again, her voice steady and politely detached. He was relieved to hear her back in control. Her stubborn pride was one of the things he loved about her—it had killed him to see her plead.

"You came into the hotel lobby last week," she continued as if it were completely normal to be having a conversation with a man who was brandishing a skinning knife. "I saw you talking to our concierge."

"I've been in the hotel plenty of times," he responded. "You just didn't see me."

"I've been kept quite busy lately."

Blount laughed as he put down his knife and poured himself another glass of wine. He displayed no signs of inebriation, though—his celebration appeared to be as calculated as everything else about him. "I bet you have," he said.

"Were you behind all the problems we've had? Or was that the work of the Corbin brothers?"

Blount narrowed his eyes. "Why are you asking me about this now?"

She lifted her chin. "I understand that you plan to kill us. What harm could there be in satisfying my curiosity before you do?"

Jackson wanted to hug her. In spite of her fear, she'd injected just the right amount of haughtiness into her request. Blount was probably eager to boast. He appeared to enjoy feeling in charge.

"For a classy woman, you sure are gullible," Blount said. "Most of those problems you had were caused by your pretty-boy concierge."

Charlotte drew in her breath. "Luc?"

Blount sipped his wine, evidently relishing her shock. "He's been working with the Corbins for months. That's how they operate. When they want to acquire a hotel, they plant someone on the inside to sabotage the business until the owner is forced to sell at a bargain price. They've been running that scam in Asia for years. Luc Carter was their guy on the inside at your place."

Charlotte faltered, her chin quivering. "No," she whispered.

"It was a good setup they had going, until Carter grew a conscience."

Jackson could see how hard this was on Charlotte. He, too, had been fooled by Luc. The man's distress during the fire had seemed genuine—if he'd been having second thoughts then, it was no wonder he'd appeared so troubled. This also explained his vehemence against the Corbins during that drunken conversation at the hotel bar. "Is that why you killed him?" Jackson asked.

Blount carried his glass to the office doorway and looked into the darkness. "He wanted out and tried to go to the cops. He made the mistake of underestimating my reach."

Jackson took advantage of the lapse in Blount's attention to give his hand a sharp twist. A two-inch section of tape suddenly pulled loose, making a distinctive hollow ripping sound.

Charlotte wriggled against her bonds, using the creaking of her chair to mask the noise Jackson had made. "You're not a hotelier like the Corbins, are you, Mr. Blount?" she asked.

He turned. "No. I have other interests."

"Then I don't see why you're going to so much trouble to get my hotel."

"It's *my* hotel now, Miss Marchand. You people never saw its potential. It will be the perfect location to expand my business. With a prestigious address like that and all those rooms to run my games and girls—"

"What does that mean?" she demanded.

"Gambling and prostitution," Jackson said. "That's what he's talking about. He's probably going to make the Hotel Marchand his headquarters."

Blount saluted him with his wineglass. "I knew you were a bright man, Dr. Bailey. That's exactly what I'll do."

Anger tightened Charlotte's lips. "I would sooner see the hotel burned to the ground than have it perverted like that. My family has put their lives into that business. They would never want any part of something so sordid."

"Your family?" Blount sneered. "Let me tell you about them, Miss High-and-Mighty Marchand. It was because of your family that I noticed the hotel. It should have been mine more than four years ago."

"I don't understand."

"I've had to put up with people like you Marchands all my life. You think because I grew up on the bayou and worked with my hands you're better than me, but I get the last laugh. I've made a fortune separating fools like your family from their money. Your uncle couldn't get enough of my games. Poker was his choice."

"My uncle? Who are you talking about?"

"Did you forget about your Uncle Pierre?"

"Pierre?" She strained forward. "*Mon Dieu*, what do you know about him? Where is he?"

Jackson eased apart another length of tape. He wanted them to keep talking, but he was concerned about Charlotte. She'd barely had a chance to deal with one blow before she was being dealt another. He'd heard of Pierre Robichaux, the black sheep of Anne's family. The man had disappeared well before Charlotte was born, driven out of his home in disgrace by Celeste.

"He's dead now," Blount said. "But not before I got what I wanted out of him."

Charlotte's eyes filled with a renewed wave of tears. She bit down on her lower lip, stubbornly refusing to let her tears fall.

"I knew Pierre's family had money," Blount continued. "That's why I let him keep losing. He got into me for a million before I called in his markers. I thought he'd go to his rich mama to bail him out, but he didn't. He went to your papa. Didn't make any difference to me who gave me the money as long as I got it."

The pieces clicked in Jackson's mind at the same time they must have fitted together in Charlotte's. She gasped. "My father transferred a million dollars to the Cayman Islands just before he died," she said. "Are you saying that went to *you?*"

"Remy was a real stand-up guy. Paid off his brother-in-law's debts without blinking as soon as I threatened to kill him." Blount snickered. "He knuckled under almost as fast as your mama did today."

"Oh, good Lord," Charlotte murmured, still trying to come to grips with it. "The money was for Uncle Pierre. Mama never knew."

"I figured with you Marchands down that much cash, the hotel would be up for grabs in no time." Blount pointed at Charlotte. "I don't know how you and your mother kept it going, but it's mine now. And it's about time. I've been a patient man."

"You *cochon*," Charlotte said through her teeth. "You've been preying on my family."

Blount drained his wineglass, placed it on his desk and retrieved his knife. "Your father was easy prey. So were your
uncle and your cousin. And your insults don't bother me. I'd
rather be a rich pig than a dead fool."

"My cousin?" Charlotte asked. "What—"

"Ah, that's right, you didn't know about that either." Blount
smiled. "You're a bigger fool than you realize. You never
guessed that Luc Carter was your cousin."

"Luc?"

"Sweet, isn't it? He hated you Marchands so much he
would have brought you down for free."

More pieces clicked in Jackson's head. Luc was Charlotte's cousin. It had been the Marchands and Celeste Robichaux he'd been talking about in the bar; *they* were the family
he'd blamed for his father's failure. Of course! Pierre had been
born rich, his mother had kicked him out—it all fit. Now
those ramblings made sense.

Too bad he hadn't made the connection before, Jackson
thought. Charlotte looked as if she'd been punched. Her
breathing was fast and shallow—she was nearing the end of
her control. "Luc wanted to tell you the truth, Charlotte," he
said, longing for some way to comfort her. "He wanted to be
part of your family."

She swung her head toward him. "You *knew*?"

"Not who he was, just that he regretted what he'd done."

"Again, this is all very touching," Mike said. "But it makes
no difference. You're all going to end up in the same place."

Jackson wrenched his hand sideways, sending shards of pain
through his wrist and up his arm. The tape was loosening—he
could feel space between his knuckles—but the progress was

too slow. Blount's boasting was taking on an air of finality, not a good sign. "You're going to need someone to run the hotel," Jackson said. "If you want to use it as a front, you'll need to keep up its reputation. Charlotte's the best manager—"

"Nice try, Doctor, but I have no further use for Miss Marchand." Mike returned to the doorway. "I only put people I can trust on my payroll."

How much time had passed since the phone call to Anne? Jackson wondered. Whoever Blount had sent to pick up the signed contract could be returning at any moment—that had to be what he kept watching for. Jackson felt a bead of sweat snake down his temple as he concentrated on closing his hand into a fist. The tape stretched, ripping apart another half inch.

A sudden shout came from the darkness beyond the office doorway. It sounded like Richard. Blount stepped onto the landing of the staircase, his attention caught by something in the shadows.

Jackson fumbled to get his fingers under the remaining tape and focused on the small revolver that Richard had left on the desk. He knew all about guns, but he'd never held one. He'd seen too much of the damage they could do to consider firing one for sport. He'd never considered intentionally harming another human being either, but he'd meant every word of his threat to Richard. He would do whatever he needed in order to save Charlotte.

More shouts echoed from the warehouse floor, along with the sound of running footsteps. There was a rapid series of gunshots.

Charlotte looked at Jackson, her eyes shining with the first gleam of hope he'd seen since he'd come to. "It must be the police," she whispered. "Oh, Jackson, we're going to make it!"

The steel staircase rang with the tread of a heavy man. Blount backed into the office as a familiar jovial face appeared in the doorway.

It was Detective Fergusson, his badge pinned to the outside of his jacket and a large automatic pistol gripped competently in his hand.

Jackson tipped back his head and exhaled in relief, glad that he'd underestimated the cop's abilities.

"Thank God," Charlotte breathed.

"Any trouble, Otis?" Blount asked.

"No problems, Mike," Fergusson said. "The Corbins are taken care of. I had to shoot them when they resisted arrest. Is that Richard's gun?"

Jackson's blood froze. No. God, *no!*

"That's it. His prints are on it," Blount replied. "It's the same one he used to shoot Carter, so this should wrap everything up in a nice, neat package."

Fergusson holstered his own gun, pulled a pair of latex gloves from his jacket pocket and slipped them on. "Thanks, Mike. I could get that commendation yet."

Charlotte began to tremble. "Detective Fergusson?" she asked. "What's going on?"

It was Blount who replied. "My old friend Otis is helping me get rid of those loose ends I mentioned."

Fergusson picked up the revolver. "The Corbin brothers have been responsible for a regular crime wave at the Hotel Marchand, culminating in a daring kidnapping." He pointed the gun at Charlotte. "Unfortunately I didn't arrive in time to stop them from killing their hostages."

CHAPTER THIRTEEN

CHARLOTTE HAD OFTEN heard that before a person died, their life flashed before their eyes. Hers didn't. No, she didn't see any orderly mental snapshots of memorable events or people. All she saw was a haze of rage.

Not now! she screamed in her head. This couldn't be her fate, to die like this. It wasn't fair. Not when she'd finally figured everything out. She rocked forward suddenly, using the weight of the metal chair for momentum to carry her to her feet.

"Charlie, get down!" Jackson yelled, surging past her.

The realization that he'd managed to free himself sent her pulse soaring. But layers of duct tape still bound her arms to her chair. She couldn't straighten up, so she lowered her head and ran at Fergusson.

Jackson got there before her. He grabbed Fergusson's arm and swung the gun aside a split second before Charlotte rammed into the cop's stomach.

The collision with his bulk knocked her backward. She reeled, trying to stay on her feet, when the legs of her chair swung into something solid.

Blount cursed, and the knife he had been holding went skidding across the floor. Charlotte was shoved forward. Unable to keep her balance, she fell to her knees. She tried to scramble up, but without the use of her hands, her stocking feet slid out from under her, sending her down hard on her side.

Footsteps sounded on the staircase and shouts came from the darkness outside. "FBI," someone yelled. "Freeze!"

A gun went off close by. The noise was followed by the thudding punch of flesh on flesh and the crunch of bone. Charlotte lifted her head, twisting her torso in an attempt to see what was happening behind her.

Men in helmets and bulletproof vests crowded through the doorway, their weapons leveled. Mike Blount raised his hands and clasped them behind his head just as Detective Fergusson dropped his gun, staggered sideways a few steps and slumped to the floor. Other details registered in some part of Charlotte's mind, but as soon as she saw Jackson, nothing else mattered.

Pieces of duct tape dangled from his wrists, the bruises on his face were darkening to violet, but he was still on his feet. He was all right.

"Jackson!" she cried.

Before his name got past her lips, he was kneeling on the floor beside her, his hand on her shoulder and his face pressed to hers. "Are you okay?"

She nodded against his cheek, gasping for breath. There was so much to say, but her throat was too tight for speech. They were alive. She would get another chance. That was all that really mattered.

He ripped away the tape that bound her. The chair clattered to the floor as he pulled her into his arms. She couldn't tell whether the trembling she felt was his or her own.

"You're safe, Charlie," he said. "No one's going to hurt you now."

A radio crackled. "Send an ambulance," someone said. "We have multiple gunshot victims."

Charlotte anchored her fingers in Jackson's shirt. Fergusson's gun—no, Richard's gun—was less than two feet away. Blount's knife gleamed in the shadow under the desk. She belatedly realized she must have knocked it out of his grasp when she'd stumbled into him with her chair. Her teeth started to chatter as the full scope of what had happened hit her. She ducked her head, seeking the hollow of Jackson's shoulder, needing the reassurance of his touch more than she needed air.

He'd risked his life for her. He'd even offered his own life to spare hers. She hadn't thought it was possible to love him more, but she did.

"You're safe," he repeated. "Look." He shifted his hold, turning her so she could see past him. "They won't hurt anyone."

Secure in the shelter of Jackson's embrace, Charlotte watched the scene unfold. Blount was handcuffed and led away by a pair of men in dark blue windbreakers with *FBI* emblazoned across the back in white letters. Someone must have switched on the warehouse lights—the glass wall of the office gleamed with reflected brightness. Sirens sounded in the distance, along with more voices, but she couldn't hear anyone running now.

Several uniformed New Orleans police officers had surrounded Fergusson. He was still on the floor where he'd fallen, moaning and clutching his nose. Blood trickled between his fingers and soaked his white mustache, yet no one was making a move to help him. Not even Jackson.

"It's okay," Jackson said, rubbing his mouth against her hair. "It's all over."

His words made her shiver. "Oh, *God!* It was so close. Are you okay, Jackson? Is your head still aching? Does your hand hurt?"

"Don't worry about me. I'm fine."

She leaned back to look for herself, but she didn't get past his lips.

The kiss was as natural as drawing breath. She closed her eyes and drank in the taste of him, driving back the fear that still clouded her mind.

And in spite of the cold floor, the milling police and FBI agents, the din of radios and men's voices, Charlotte felt a sense of rightness, as if everything was finally settling into place.

"Miss Marchand? Dr. Bailey?"

Jackson touched his forehead to hers. "We'll finish this later, Charlie," he whispered.

"Jackson—"

"I promise," he said.

A man in plain clothes had separated from the rest of the police and was approaching them. The face seemed familiar. A second later, Charlotte recognized him. It was the policeman who had dealt with the death of a hotel guest several weeks earlier. Renee had mentioned that she was trying to contact him. "Detective Rothberg!"

He held out his hand to them. "I apologize for the late arrival. Do either of you need medical attention?"

Charlotte hiccuped, unable to think of a coherent response. Did he have to sound so…polite?

Jackson gave her a kiss on the cheek, then slipped his arm around her waist and helped her to stand. "No, we're all right."

"That's some punch you pack for a doctor," Rothberg said. "It looks as if you broke Otis's nose."

Punch? Charlotte glanced at Fergusson again as she replayed the sounds of those last frantic moments. The blood on his face was coming from his nose. He hadn't been shot; Jackson had hit him.

"If you don't mind," Rothberg continued, "I'd like to ask both of you some questions. The FBI would like to speak with you, too."

"We'd be happy to cooperate after we've gotten some rest," Jackson said firmly. "What we need right now is a ride home."

Rothberg appeared as if he were about to argue, then stepped back to confer with one of the FBI agents. Nodding curtly, he gestured toward the door. Charlotte and Jackson followed Rothberg out of the office and down to the warehouse floor, where paramedics were beginning to work on Dan and Richard Corbin. The entrance to the street stood wide open. Through it came the flicker of lights from emergency vehicles, as well as the pink tinge of dawn.

It was already morning. In one way, Charlotte couldn't believe so much time had passed. Yet in another, the night had seemed endless. She was grateful that Jackson had delayed the interviews with the authorities—she should have been exhausted, but her nerves were jumping as if she'd overdosed on caffeine.

Rothberg spoke briefly with some of the officers who were outside, then led Charlotte and Jackson to one of the police cars that were parked in front of the warehouse. Farther down the street, a long black limousine stood with its doors open. Two more police cruisers, their light bars still flashing, were angled against its front and rear bumpers.

Charlotte hung on more tightly to Jackson as an image of their abduction stole through her mind. "That looks like the limo the Corbins were using when they kidnapped us."

"It belongs to Mike Blount," Rothberg said, opening the rear door of the police car. "Vice has been after him for years, but he's always skated through the charges, primarily because he doesn't leave witnesses."

"Blount was waiting for his driver to bring the ransom," Jackson said. "Is that how you found us, by trailing him here?"

"No, we were acting on a tip from a man we have in custody. We arrived in time to stop Blount's driver, but unfortunately we were too late to intercept Detective Fergusson."

Charlotte paused in the angle of the open door. "Is my mother all right? I have to tell her we're safe. This must have been a terrible strain on her heart."

"Mrs. Marchand is in good health," Rothberg said. "Your mother and your sisters have been cooperating with us throughout the night. I assure you they would have heard the news of your rescue by now."

Charlotte remembered the nightmarish conversation with Blount. Letting her mother know she and Jackson were safe wasn't the only thing she had to tell her.

Some of the exhilaration of being rescued faded. She glanced at Jackson. "I don't know how I'll be able to break the news about Pierre. Mama doesn't know he's dead. She loved him so much."

"Anne's a strong woman, Charlotte," Jackson said. "She'll be able to handle it."

"He was her baby brother. I can't imagine losing any of my sisters. And what about Luc? It's going to devastate Mama to learn that he died before we got the chance to know who he was. It will hurt her even more to find out that he betrayed us."

"But he did have regrets, Charlotte. If Luc had lived—"

"Luc?" Rothberg interrupted. "Do you mean Luc Carter, the hotel concierge who was shot?"

Jackson nodded. "He tried to warn us about the plot against Charlotte."

"Yes, the paramedics related that to us."

"Blount had him killed because he wanted to turn himself in."

"But he wasn't killed, Dr. Bailey," Rothberg said. "He's in our custody at Mercy Hospital."

Charlotte grasped the top of the car door, her knees suddenly wobbly. "What? Luc's alive?"

"Yes, the last I heard. It's been touch and go. He wasn't able to talk to anyone until an hour ago, but he had a lot to say when he did. He's the one who told us where to find you."

JACKSON LEANED BACK against the corridor wall, cradled his hand against his chest to relieve the ache and watched Charlotte through the window of the ICU. On the surface she bore little resemblance to the elegantly polished woman he'd first seen in the hotel courtyard a week ago. Her clothes were wrinkled and streaked with dirt. Instead of high heels, she wore a pair of hospital-issue cloth slippers. She'd washed her face and tried to smooth her hair when they'd arrived at the hospital, but whatever straightening product she'd used before was wearing off, because the ends had reverted to her natural curls.

That was Charlotte. Stubborn to the core. Even her hair had a mind of its own.

He clenched his jaw, caught between a groan and a laugh.

After what she'd been through in the past twenty-four hours, she belonged in bed. They both did. He'd tried to get her there, but he'd known she wouldn't rest until she'd stopped in to see Luc.

She pulled a chair closer to the IV pole and reached for Luc's hand where it lay on the covers. The nurses had cautioned her not to disturb him—talking to the police earlier had sapped his strength—so she didn't try to wake him up. She simply didn't want him to be alone.

That was Charlotte, too. Her sense of loyalty to her family ran deep. It defined who she was. It had been one of the things that had kept her and Jackson apart, but in fact, it was one of the things he'd always loved about her.

There was a soft chime from one of the elevators down the hall. Jackson turned his head in time to see Charlotte's sisters step out of the car. Melanie spotted him first and hurried forward. "Jackson!" She grasped his arm as she stretched up to kiss his cheek. "I'm so glad you're okay." She focused on his bruises and shuddered. "You *are* okay, aren't you?"

"More or less."

"I still can't believe everything that's happened. Where's Charlotte?"

"In there," he said, nodding toward the glass-walled room on the other side of the corridor.

Melanie turned. "I can't believe that part either. Is it true? Luc's our cousin?"

Sylvie and Renee reached Jackson together, each engulfing him in a firm hug before they echoed their youngest sister's questions. Charlotte had given them only the bare details over the phone, so Jackson added what he knew.

He could see varying degrees of anger on their faces, which was understandable in view of how Luc had deliberately set out to hurt the family through the hotel. Like Charlotte, they might accept Luc as part of the family, yet it was going to take time for the gulf he'd created to heal.

Sylvie glanced at the police officer who sat in a chair outside the entrance to the ICU. "Jackson, is Luc going to face charges?"

"It's possible," Jackson replied. "He didn't ask for a deal before he talked to the police. His priority was saving our lives."

Melanie stepped up to the glass and studied Luc. "We all make mistakes," she said. "It takes courage to admit them."

"Luc was shot because he tried to change," Sylvie said, moving beside Melanie. "He wanted to do the right thing. He told the truth even though it got him arrested."

"That has to count for something," Melanie said.

Unlike her younger sisters, Renee didn't say anything in Luc's defense. Her expression was hopeful but guarded as she looked at Jackson. "He's going to be all right, isn't he?"

Jackson turned to assess the young man on the hospital bed. His face was pale and his body lax. Along with the IV that was connected to his arm, he was hooked up to monitors that tracked his respiration and heart rate. He didn't bear much resemblance to the handsome blond concierge Jackson had first met a week ago.

According to the E.R. doctors, Luc had been close to death by the time he'd reached the hospital. Jackson's initial guess had been right—the bullet had nicked Luc's liver, and the massive internal bleeding had nearly proven fatal. Somehow, though, Luc had found the will to live through surgery. Now that the damage had been repaired and the blood he'd lost replaced, he was expected to make a full recovery.

Then again, Luc's survival wasn't that unexpected. After all, he was related to the Marchands. Strength seemed to run in the family.

"He'll make it," Jackson said. He looked at Charlotte. "He wants a second chance, and that gives a man a lot to live for."

As if she could feel his gaze, she glanced toward the glass. She smiled and rose from the chair.

Her sisters surrounded her as soon as she stepped into the corridor. Jackson stayed where he was, not wanting to intrude on the reunion. Charlotte's eyes were moist again—she'd been crying on and off for most of the night—but these were healing tears.

It was just as well that they'd made this detour instead of going straight to Charlotte's house. He'd seen the aftereffects of trauma far too often and he knew that victims needed love and reassurance to heal emotionally as much as they needed physical comfort. A phone call from the police wouldn't have been enough for Charlotte's family, either. They needed to see her in person.

The elevator chimed again. Anne Marchand stepped out, but she wasn't alone. A tall silver-haired man moved beside her. Dressed in pyjamas and a burgundy dressing gown, William Armstrong nevertheless managed to look as dignified as if he were wearing one of his typical suits.

Jackson strode toward them. William had been allowed out of bed for a few days now but only for short, supervised walks. "Uncle William. Do the nurses on duty know you've left your floor?"

Anne put her arms around her fiancé's waist. "See, William? I'm not the only one who's worried. There was no reason for you to meet me."

"There was every reason," he said, taking another careful step forward. He had one arm draped around Anne's shoulders, but most of his weight was on the cane he gripped in his right hand. "I've been here over a week. You've already had to face too much on your own."

Jackson assessed his uncle's condition, automatically gauging his color and the rate of the pulse he could see in the vein on the side of his neck. There was a slight tremor in William's arm from the effort of leaning on his cane, but his steps were steady. He was right—it had been more than a week since his surgery. As long as he didn't overdo it, the walk would be beneficial.

Yet even if Jackson had wanted to object, one look into William's eyes told him his uncle wouldn't have listened. Jackson recognized that expression. This was a man in love. If William thought Anne needed him, he would be with her no matter what the cost.

By the time they reached Luc's room Renee had gone inside to take her turn sitting with her cousin. Anne released William to pull Charlotte into a hard embrace. They clung to each other in silence, parent to child, woman to woman, confirming the bond they would share for life. Yet when Anne finally pulled back, her joy at seeing her daughter safe was clouded by grief. "Oh, *chérie*, I was so worried." She looked at Jackson. "About both of you."

"I'm sorry about Pierre, Mama," Charlotte said. "I wish the news was only good."

"Shh, *bébé*, don't fret. I would have heard about my brother soon anyway. William had people looking for him."

"I'm not going to call off their investigation yet," William said. "I'm sure you'll want to learn all you can."

"Thank you, darling. You know me so well." Anne moved her gaze to the window. She studied her nephew for a while. "I hope to know Luc someday, too. I liked him from the beginning."

"We all did," Charlotte said. "He's a charming young man."

"I wonder if some part of me recognized Pierre in him."

"He doesn't look anything like your brother, as far as I can remember," William said.

Anne continued to regard Luc. "I know, but it's more than that. There's a certain air about him that I recognize in here," she said, tapping her fingertips to her chest. "It's hard to explain. It's almost as if…" Her voice hitched. "This is going to sound silly."

"What, Mama?" Charlotte asked.

"Well, regardless of what Luc had planned to do when he came to the hotel, this was how things were meant to happen. Perhaps fate was trying to bring Pierre's son home to us all along."

At Anne's comment, Sylvie moved away from where she'd been standing near the window and slipped her arm around her mother's shoulders. "Of course fate had a hand in this, Mama. After all, it *is* Mardi Gras. Anything can happen."

Charlotte pressed her fingertips to her temples. "I completely forgot what day it is."

"Well, you have been rather busy," Sylvie said.

"There's so much to do," Charlotte said. "Julie must be swamped. And if you're here, Sylvie, who's managing the art gallery?" She twisted to look at Melanie. "Doesn't Robert need help with the preparations for the ball? That menu you planned is so ambitious. And Renee should be coordinating the event team. This is the most important night of the year for us." Her outburst stopped as quickly as it had started. She glanced down at her soiled clothes, then looked at Jackson. "It's Mardi Gras."

He'd been wondering when reality would set in. He'd hoped to get her home first, for her sake as much as for his. Her adrenaline had already worn off and her body would be needing sleep. His motives for wanting to get her alone weren't entirely selfish.

Who was he kidding? Of course his motives were selfish. He wanted to grab her and kiss her until she forgot about everything except him. Or, better yet, throw her over his shoulder and carry her away from her family and the hotel, have her all to himself again.

But if he wanted a second chance with Charlotte, that wasn't the way to go about it. He took a steadying breath, determined to keep his voice level even if it killed him. "Yes, it's Mardi Gras."

"You need to see Yves."

Her remark caught him off guard. "That can wait."

"No, it can't. This is why you came home." She looked at her mother. "I'm sorry, but you'll all have to manage without me today."

"Of course, *chérie*," Anne said. "After what you've been through, no one expects you to go to work."

"Good, because I have other priorities." She caught Jackson's arm. "We'll have to call Yves and Marie and tell them to wait for us. We can stop by my house and change clothes on the way."

"Charlotte, I don't need Yves to run the test. I know what the result will be."

In spite of the weariness that tinged the corners of her eyes, her expression turned fierce. She said goodbye to her family and walked to the elevator with him, her cloth slippers slapping briskly against the floor. She didn't speak again until she had punched in the button for the lobby and they were on their way down. "We're not giving up. Things worked out for the hotel, they'll work out for you."

"That's what I'm hoping, but it has nothing to do with my hand."

"It does. I know how much this means to you. We'll do whatever it takes—"

"Charlotte, look," he said, holding up his right hand.

"Mon Dieu!" she whispered. "It's so swollen. What's wrong? How…?" She sucked in her breath. "The tape! You hurt yourself when you tried to get loose, didn't you? Why didn't you say anything sooner?"

Jackson had planned to wait until later before he revealed what had happened. Charlotte had needed to focus on her family and she'd already had enough shocks to deal with.

But he knew her well enough to realize she wouldn't be put off any longer. He reached past her to press the emergency stop on the elevator, and the car jerked to a halt. "Take a closer look," he said, squeezing his hand into a fist.

"Your knuckles are red. They look so sore." She touched her fingertips to his hand. "We should have gone straight to Emergency instead of going to see Luc. Maybe it isn't too late…."

Her words trailed off as she finally took in what she was seeing. "Jackson, you made a fist."

"I was showing off." He dropped his hand and shook it out. "I can't do it for long. It aches like hell."

"It *aches?* You can feel it?"

"I can feel everything."

"My God." Her eyes widened. "You hit Fergusson with your *right* hand. That's why your knuckles are red."

"I had to. I was hanging on to his gun arm with my left. I couldn't let him get off another shot."

"But how…?" She reached for his hand and held it gingerly between both of hers, just as she had countless times during the past week. "This is incredible."

His fingers still felt as if they were surrounded by glass shards, but the warmth of Charlotte's touch soothed the pain, so he didn't pull away. "Yves said there could have been bone fragments in the way that might have been interfering with the healing process."

"Yes, I remember! Do you think…?"

"The best I can figure, all the straining I did while I was trying to get out of the tape ripped something loose inside the scar tissue."

"Oh, Jackson, this is just marvelous." Her voice broke. Once again her eyes brimmed with tears. "I'm so happy for you."

"I've still got a long way to go before I can even think about picking up a scalpel. This is just the start."

"You'll make it. I know you will."

"So will you, Charlotte. Your hotel is safe now. I understand how you love that place."

She wiped her cheeks on the back of his hand. She didn't reply.

Jackson knew they should be happy. Against all odds, they'd both won.

Yet Charlotte was starting to tremble again, and her tears were flowing faster.

"Don't cry, Charlie. Whatever happens today, you won't lose the hotel. It could take a while, but with the right lawyer, you might be able to get back some of the million Remy transferred to Blount's bank. Your insurance agent will have to pay your claim for the fire, too. Everything's going to be fine."

She licked a tear from the corner of her mouth and smiled, but the smile didn't reach her eyes. She turned and pressed the button to restart the elevator. "Yes, we're both going to get what we want."

CHAPTER FOURTEEN

CHARLOTTE WOKE UP WITH her pulse pounding. The shade was drawn and the bedroom curtains were closed—she couldn't see any daylight—and for an instant she thought she was back in that windowless closet in Blount's warehouse....

But then she felt Jackson's breath stir her hair, and the length of his body warmed her back as his arm slid around her waist.

And she knew without a doubt that she was home.

"Finally," Jackson murmured. He moved her hair aside and kissed the back of her neck. "It's about time you woke up."

She exhaled shakily. "The room's so dark. What time is it?"

"It's still afternoon. Last time I checked my watch it was almost three." He kissed his way to her ear. "I meant to ask you, why don't you have an alarm clock in your bedroom?"

"I tried, but I always ended up turning it off and going back to sleep, so I keep it in the kitchen now."

"Ah, I should have guessed. It's that morning-person issue again."

She arched her neck as he kissed her earlobe. Of all the things she wanted to talk about, the time of day wasn't one of them.

Yet neither of them had felt like talking when they'd finally reached her house. A bath, then bed had been all she'd had the energy for. Even their lovemaking had been quieter than usual.

Or maybe she hadn't said anything because she'd been putting this off. She'd known it was going to hurt.

She closed her eyes, trying to recapture the resolve she'd felt this morning. "Jackson?"

He eased her onto her back and kissed the corner of her jaw. "Mmm?"

"You're still going to see Yves, aren't you?"

"I rescheduled the appointment for tomorrow."

"When did you do that?"

"I phoned him while you were sleeping."

"Did you tell him about your hand?"

"Uh-huh."

"Did he agree with your diagnosis?"

He gave her a gentle bite on her shoulder. "Charlie, could you pay attention here? I'm trying to seduce you."

Oh, she knew what he was trying to do, and he was doing a good job, too. It didn't take much for him to make her body respond. What harm would there be if she stayed where she was and let this happen….

No. That's what she'd been doing all along. She wriggled out from underneath him to switch on the lamp, then slid out of bed and pulled on her robe. "Please, just answer my question. It's important."

Sighing, he stretched out on his side. The sheet bunched at his waist, leaving his chest bare, revealing every ripple of muscle as he flexed his arm and propped his head on his left hand. Charlotte was close—oh so close—to sliding back into bed when he held out his right hand. "Yves doesn't want to agree until he sees it for himself."

"He's optimistic, though, isn't he?"

Jackson chuckled. "He whooped so loudly when I told him, my ear's still ringing. Marie is convinced it was because of her gris-gris. I didn't tell her I never took it out of the package."

She watched him move his fingers. Although his motions were stiff, they were strong. The wonder of what had happened was still difficult to fathom, yet the truth of it was undeniable. Jackson was healing.

She tied the belt of her robe and knelt on the mattress to face him. "It's the best news we could possibly hear."

"Hey." He rubbed his knuckle beneath her eye. "You're not going to start crying again, are you?"

"I never cry."

"Sure. You don't yell either."

"No, that would be rude."

"And you're too much of a lady to head-butt a cop three times your size while you're wearing a chair taped to your back, right?"

Hearing him joke about the nightmare helped to put it in perspective. She smiled. That was her Jackson. He always knew what she needed. "You're the one who saved our lives. If you hadn't managed to free yourself…"

"I couldn't have done that if you hadn't kept Blount distracted. You were amazing."

"It's surprising what we're capable of given the right motivation, isn't it?"

He made a fist again, then spread his fingers wide. "I couldn't have said it better myself. We make a good team, Charlie."

"Yes, Jackson," she murmured. "We do. That's what I want to talk to you about."

"Oh?"

"Did Yves say anything about surgery or possible treatment?"

"We didn't get that far. Why?"

She took a steadying breath and said it all at once. "I wanted to know how long you'll be staying in New Orleans."

He dropped his hand to the mattress. It was a while before he responded. "Why? Are you kicking me out?"

"Of course I'm not kicking you out! I plan to come with you when you leave."

There was another silence. In the subdued light from the draped window and the bedside lamp the bruises on Jackson's face looked more like shadows. His hair had still been damp from their bath when they'd gotten into bed, and had dried in wild tufts all over his head. He was, Charlotte decided, truly the handsomest man she had ever seen.

Especially when he smiled, as he did now. "You plan to come with me," he repeated.

She traced the outline of his hand with her fingertip. "I know this isn't what we agreed on, Jackson, but—"

"Agreed on?" He sat up. "Did I miss something?"

"We had the conversation right here," she said, pointing at the mattress. "We said that what was going on between us was only sex and that nothing had to change. We're two consenting adults under stress and—"

"You don't believe that, do you?"

"It's what you said."

"Sure, that's what I said, but I was wrong. There's no way either of us can pretend what's going on between us is just sex or chemistry." He stopped and shook his head. "I thought I was keeping things simple, but they already were, only I was too stubborn to see it."

"What?"

He shifted to kneel in front of her and took her hands in his. "What's going on between us is the simplest thing in the world. I should know, because I've seen it in one form or another everywhere I've traveled. It's the true source of the strength people need to survive. It's love, Charlie. I love you."

The words had been trapped in her head so long it took her a moment to realize he'd been the one to say them. "You love me?"

His smile brought out the dimple in his cheek, blending the boy with the man. He moved his hands to her shoulders and leaned closer. "You'd really come with me?"

Now she didn't understand why she'd hesitated so long. Yes, there would be pain, but it would heal. "Absolutely. Just because we can't change the past doesn't mean we have to repeat it."

"You'd leave your home?"

She put her palm on his chest over his heart. "When I'm with you, Jackson, I *am* home."

His fingers tightened. All of his fingers. "What about the hotel?"

"That's why I need to know when you're leaving. I have to train my replacement."

"Charlie, I couldn't ask you to do that. You love that place."

"It's just a building," she said. "I can't love a building the way I can love a person."

"If you're trying to say what I think you are, you're sure going about it in a convoluted way."

She leaned forward to kiss him. This was getting easier by the second. "Fine. You want me to make it official? Yes, Jackson Bailey, I love you."

He grinned. "Then let's both make it official. My first marriage proposal's still open—"

The next kiss wasn't quick. It had been waiting for twenty years, and the answer was unmistakable. Jackson wrapped his arms around her back and pulled her down to the bed on top of him. The familiar tingles that he'd triggered when she'd awakened returned with a strength that stole her breath.

But this time it was Jackson who stopped. He rolled them to their sides and eased back to look at her. His gaze sparked with passion, but his lips were twitching with humor. "Damn! Do you realize what we're doing?"

She trailed her fingers down his stomach. "I have a pretty good idea."

He grasped her hand and carried it to his lips. He smiled as he kissed her knuckles. "Aside from that."

"Mmm?"

"It's the watch all over again."

"What watch? I don't really care what time it is—"

"No, Charlie, remember my watch? The one that got tangled in your hair when we were kids?"

She blinked. "I remember. We talked about that last week."

"I wouldn't let you cut your hair and you wouldn't let me break my watch."

"Yes, but what—"

"That's what's happening. Charlie, I don't want you to give up the hotel."

"I'm not staying behind. Even if I do have to live in a tent part of the year."

"I love you for offering." He kissed her nose. "But we're not going anywhere."

"But your work overseas is important. You love it."

"New Orleans needs doctors, too."

"You said you hate it here, that you could never be happy."

He kissed her forehead and both of her cheeks. "It wasn't the place I hated, it was how it made me feel. Believe it or not, I've grown up since then. I don't have anything to prove. And how could I be jealous of your family? It was their love that helped form you into the woman *I* love."

This was too much to take in. She'd been fully prepared to start a new life somewhere else if that's what Jackson had needed. "Are you sure?"

"It wasn't only Yves I phoned while you were sleeping. He gave me the names of some people to contact about setting up a charity clinic here. With the rebuilding still going on, the need is greater than ever."

"Jackson, that's…" She struggled for a word. Nothing seemed adequate. Laughing, she grasped his face between her palms. "I love you."

"Then does this mean I have your attention?"

"What?"

"As I recall, I was in the middle of seducing you."

It was a long time before either of them felt the need to speak again. By then, Charlotte had realized which word she had sought.

Perfect.

EPILOGUE

"AUNTIE CHARLOTTE! Make a wish."

Charlotte turned just as Daisy Rose barreled into her skirt. She leaned down to help extricate her from the yards of blue satin, then straightened her niece's wings. "Are you sure you have any magic left in that wand, *chérie?*"

"Tons," Daisy Rose said. She whipped the end back and forth. The gold-painted star turned into a glittering streak. "See?"

Jackson slipped his arm around Charlotte's waist. "Sure looks to me as if it's still loaded. What are you going to wish for, Charlie?"

"Now that's a tough question. What don't I have?" She pursed her lips and laid her finger against her cheek. "Maybe another day off?"

Daisy Rose tapped the wand against Charlotte's arm. "Your wish is grannied."

"Grannied?"

"She means granted," Sylvie said, squeezing through the crowd to join them. She took a tissue from her sleeve and squatted to wipe a smear of chocolate from Daisy Rose's mouth. Sylvie's gown was made from the same spangled yellow tulle as her daughter's, and both of them looked as if they floated on air. "I didn't think you two were going to make it."

"If either of us knew how to cook, we might not have," Jackson said. "But since Robert and Melanie went to all this trouble, the least we could do is help eat."

Charlotte laughed and dug an elbow into his side. "Don't listen to him. We wouldn't have missed this celebration for anything."

"We do have a lot to celebrate," Jefferson said as he extended his hand to help Sylvie up. "This is one Mardi Gras none of us will forget."

Sylvie gave a private smile to her fiancé before she turned back to Charlotte. "You look fabulous. That gown is so…you."

"Genevieve's a true artist." Charlotte pinched a fold of the skirt and swept it toward her niece so the feathers at the hem tickled her nose.

Daisy Rose giggled and whipped her wand back and forth again.

"Better grab her before she reloads that thing," Jackson said.

Jefferson took Daisy Rose by the hands and twirled her toward him. "Climb on," he said, guiding her to step onto the toes of his shoes. "I believe this is our dance."

Charlotte leaned her head on Jackson's shoulder and swayed to the beat as Jefferson waltzed off with Sylvie and Daisy Rose. The music was a lively blend of fiddles and accordions—Renee had settled on a Cajun band in honor of their father's roots. It had been a good choice. The upbeat tempo wove through the crowd as effortlessly as laughter.

There was plenty of that in the room tonight. The hotel was full to capacity, and the guests were enjoying themselves almost as much as the Marchand family. Renee's crew had transformed the event rooms into a fairy-tale meadow, straight out of Charlotte's favorite book. Strings of tiny lights twinkled from the ceiling, and fanciful painted plywood creatures watched from the greenery. A miniature castle, complete with turrets and a drawbridge, had been assembled in the far corner, while a fog machine sent wisps of enchantment curling along the floor.

The walls of the Hotel Marchand were once again echoing with good memories.

Only a week ago Charlotte had been dreading this ball. She'd thought that things couldn't have gotten any worse. Now she couldn't imagine them getting any better.

Jackson rubbed his thumb along her midriff. "Do you still want one of those?"

"What?"

"A child."

Her eyes filled. Oh, yes. Things could indeed get better. She tipped her head back to look at Jackson. "I realize this is what I talked about twenty years ago, but I'm forty years old now."

"I don't think dreams come with an expiration date, Charlie. We're living proof of that."

"The chances aren't that good."

"After everything we've been through, are you really going to pay any attention to the odds?"

She smiled. "Unless you want me to start crying again, we'll have to talk about this later."

He moved his hand to the satin over her hip as he guided her to the dance floor. "I look forward to doing more than talking."

"So that's what this is about," she said on a laugh. "You just don't want to bother stopping at the drugstore to buy another box of—"

"Charlotte Anne."

The voice smothered her laughter as quickly as a wet towel. She automatically straightened her spine. "*Grand-mère*. I'm so glad to see that you decided to attend."

In spite of the party going on around her, Celeste Robichaux appeared to stand in a circle of calm. She was a small woman, yet her bearing carried a presence that set her apart. Dressed in purple damask, her silver hair coiled in her trademark French roll, she gestured toward Jackson with the tip of her cane. "I was told that you had returned."

Charlotte knew that Jackson wasn't the same insecure boy he'd once been—he didn't need to prove anything to Celeste—yet she felt herself bristling at her grandmother's disapproving regard.

Before she could say anything, Jackson stepped forward and kissed Celeste on both cheeks. "You're looking well, Miss Celeste."

"Thank you. We have certain standards we must maintain on occasions such as this." She swept Jackson with a disdainful glance. "Your face is bruised like a common prizefighter's."

"My apologies," Jackson said smoothly. "I meant no offense. I'll do my best to keep my appearance from frightening the children."

Celeste's mouth twitched. She pinched her lips together and stacked her hands on her cane. "I understand you saved my granddaughter's life."

"Charlotte and I worked as a team. I'd say we saved each other."

"I've also learned that you saved my grandson's life yesterday."

"I did what I could to stabilize him. The surgeons at the hospital did the rest."

Celeste dipped her chin in a regal nod. "It appears your education was put to good use."

"I plan to put it to use here from now on," he said. He smiled at Charlotte and laced his fingers with hers. "I'll be staying in New Orleans permanently."

Celeste's hand fluttered on her cane as she looked at the two of them. "Then is it true, Charlotte? You and this…this…"

"Yes, *Grand-mère*, this Bailey boy and I plan to stay together for good."

Beneath the purple damask Celeste's shoulders seemed to droop. "Very well. Since all of your sisters have decided to become engaged, it's proper that you do, too, since you're the eldest. But I will not apologize. I acted in your best interests."

Charlotte felt Jackson tense. She squeezed his fingers gently. "Perhaps you'd better explain, *Grand-mère*."

"You two were completely unsuited to each other, so I did what was necessary to separate you."

"Miss Celeste," Jackson said. "What exactly did you do?"

The tiny woman lifted her chin quickly. "You didn't actually believe that a full scholarship to a prestigious institution such as Harvard would fall into your hands out of the blue, did you? The dean of admissions was an old friend of mine."

This was the last thing Charlotte had expected. And from the shock on Jackson's face, it had surprised him, too. She took a step toward her grandmother. "Are you claiming that you had something to do with Jackson's scholarship?"

Celeste's sharp gaze was defiant. "I provided fifty percent of the funds."

Charlotte swayed forward. "How dare you! You deliberately manipulated—"

Jackson wrapped his arms around Charlotte's waist and pulled her back to his chest. "Thank you for your generosity, Miss Celeste," he said. "You are a truly gracious and insightful lady. May we consider that an early wedding gift?"

Celeste's mouth twitched again. She rapped her cane against the floor, muttered a caution against being cheeky and swept back into the crowd. Charlotte watched her go, seething inside, until she felt the tremors in Jackson's arms. The moment she twisted to look at him, he burst into laughter.

"It's not funny!" she said. "My grandmother meddled in our lives. She deliberately broke us up."

He kissed her nose and whirled her into a waltz. "We did most of that ourselves, Charlie. But this only proves we were meant to be together."

"But—"

"Surviving the Corbins and Mike Blount is lucky enough. Saving your hotel, getting back the use of my hand, that's unbelievable. But to foil Miss Celeste—that's *really* beating the odds."

She couldn't help laughing. "I see your point."

"This was how things were meant to happen all along."

"It wasn't irony, it was fate."

"It was love, Charlie." Jackson smiled as they danced past the castle. "Makes you almost believe in magic, doesn't it?"

* * * * *

HOTEL MARCHAND
Four sisters.
A family legacy.
And someone is out to destroy it.

A new Harlequin continuity series continues in
February 2007 with
HER SUMMER LOVER
by Marissa Carroll

He was her first love...the one she's never forgotten.

Sophie Clarkson loved visiting her godmother in Louisiana's bayou country, but her most cherished memory is the enchanted summer she fell in love with Alain Boudreaux. Now chief of police and a divorced father of two, Alain had once convinced Sophie there could be no future for a big-city girl and a Cajun boy. But as Sophie starts to fall in love all over again, she realizes this is her chance to prove just how wrong he was all those years ago....

Here's a preview!

SHE SMILED. It pleased her that she remembered at least a few of the bits and pieces of Indigo history that Maude had told her over the years. One or two people passed by and nodded pleasantly, trying politely not to stare too hard. Sophie nodded back, recognizing them from the wake and the funeral, but her attention remained focused on the opera house.

The building needed painting, she realized as she drew closer, and Marjolaine and Hugh Prejean, the old gentleman she'd spoken to at the wake, were right, the roof did need work. She could see half a dozen places where the shingles were missing just from where she stood. The almost simultaneous blows of Hurricanes Katrina and Rita a couple of years earlier had damaged the old structure even more than the occupation of Union soldiers had.

Sophie turned the heavy key that had been among the items in Maude's purse in the lock and opened one of the big double doors. Once more the scents of lavender and old leather and dust tickled her nostrils, but this time her sorrow was mixed with happiness. She had always loved Past Perfect. The summer she had been so madly in love with Alain, she had imagined herself living in Indigo and working with her godmother among all these mementos of a bygone day.

Of course, when she'd gotten home to Houston, her mother had disabused her of that notion pretty quickly. And even if she'd had the courage to stand up for herself, Alain's short, curt letter breaking off their secret engagement because he had decided to enter the army to earn money for college had put an end to her girlish fantasies.

At least until that other summer, the short window of time after her divorce when she'd thought they might find that lost love again, before Alain's pregnant wife had discovered them in each other's arms.

In this very building.

The bell above the door jingled a greeting as she stepped inside. Past Perfect's showroom occupied the lobby of the opera house, a space twice as long as it was deep. The counter, a relic of a demolished Memphis department store, stood directly in front of the tall, carved double doors that led into the auditorium.

That brought her up short for a moment, but she shook off the shiver of embarrassment and remorse. She didn't have to go into the storage area with its raised stage and two tiny bow-fronted boxes high on the wall—not yet, not unless she wanted to. And she would when she wasn't thinking about Alain but of what a treasure trove of make-believe the opera house had been for a young girl. The narrow stairs to the boxes had been steep and a little scary to climb, but when she was up there looking down, her imagination had had no trouble at all turning the creaky wooden folding chair on which she perched into a velvet and gilt one. She'd populated the shabby seats below with beautiful ladies in hoop skirts and dashing gentlemen in gray uniforms with plumed hats and swords at their sides, hearing voices and music in her head that had once brought the empty space to life. Those were the memories she'd keep in her thoughts when she did venture inside.

She wandered further into the jumble of furniture and knickknacks, realizing as she always did that her godmother's seemingly haphazard arrangement of merchandise actually facilitated the flow of customer traffic, leading them eventually to the assortment of antebellum Indigo souvenirs, candles and personal-care products that brought her a good deal of income from less-than-enthusiastic antiquers and tourists who might otherwise leave the premises without taking out their wallets and credit cards.

She wondered who among her Indigo acquaintances would be qualified to take over the operation of Past Perfect. Sadly, over the past seven years, those acquaintances had dwindled to a handful. But she was getting ahead of herself, thinking about reopening the store. First she needed to have an inventory taken for estate purposes, both here and at the house.

She might as well get an idea of what she was up against.

She headed resolutely for the tall, carved doors leading into the auditorium, took a breath and twisted the handles to throw them wide. The doorbell tinkled and Sophie swiveled her head. Beyond the wavy glass, a tall man in a dark shirt and a gray Stetson was silhouetted against the bright afternoon sun. Alain. Her past had come back to haunt her.

HOTEL MARCHAND

*Four sisters. A family legacy.
And someone is out to destroy it.*

He was her first love…
the one she's never forgotten.

HER SUMMER LOVER

by

Marisa Carroll

Sophie Clarkson's most cherished memory is the
enchanted summer she fell in love with Alain Boudreaux
as a teenager. Alain had been convinced there was no future
for a big-city girl and a Cajun boy. But when a funeral
reunites them and old feelings resurface, Sophie decides to
show the lonely single father how very wrong he was.

Available February 2007.

HOTEL MARCHAND

$1.⁰⁰ OFF

The Marchand family story
continues in February with
Her Summer Lover
by Marisa Carroll.

He was her first love.
The one she'd never forgotten...

Pick up this romantic story
about a second chance at love
and get $1.⁰⁰ off.

Coupon expires May 31, 2007. Redeemable at participating retail
outlets in the U.S. only. Limit one coupon per customer.

HOTEL MARCHAND

$1.⁰⁰ OFF

The Marchand family story continues in February with *Her Summer Lover* **by Marisa Carroll.**

He was her first love.
The one she'd never forgotten…

Pick up this romantic story about a second chance at love and get $1.⁰⁰ off.

Coupon expires May 31, 2007. Redeemable at participating retail outlets in Canada only. Limit one coupon per customer.

52607598

HMCOUP07CDN

HARLEQUIN®
SuperRomance®

Is it really possible to find true love
when you're single...with kids?

Introducing an exciting new five-book miniseries,

SINGLES...WITH KIDS

When Margo almost loses her bistro...and custody of
her children...she realizes a real family is about more
than owning a pretty house and being a perfect mother.
And then there's the new man in her life, Robert...
Like the other single parents in her support group, she
has to make sure he wants the whole package.

Starting in February 2007 with

LOVE AND THE SINGLE MOM

by C.J. Carmichael

(Harlequin Superromance #1398)

ALSO WATCH FOR:

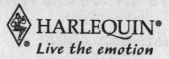

HARLEQUIN®
Live the emotion

HARLEQUIN *Romance*

What a month!

In February watch for

Rancher and Protector

Part of the Western Weddings miniseries

BY JUDY CHRISTENBERRY

The Boss's Pregnancy Proposal

BY RAYE MORGAN

Also in February, expect
MORE of what you love
as the Harlequin Romance line
increases to six titles per month.

Silhouette Desire

Don't miss the first book
in THE ROYALS trilogy:

THE FORBIDDEN PRINCESS
(SD #1780)

by national bestselling author

DAY LECLAIRE

Moments before her loveless royal wedding,
Princess Alyssa was kidnapped by a mysterious man
who'd do anything to stop the ceremony. Even if that
meant marrying the forbidden princess himself!

On sale February 2007 from Silhouette Desire!

THE ROYALS
Stories of scandals and secrets
amidst the most powerful palaces.

Make sure to read the other titles in the series:
THE PRINCE'S MISTRESS
On sale March 2007
THE ROYAL WEDDING NIGHT
On sale April 2007

*Available wherever books are sold, including most
bookstores, supermarkets, discount stores and drugstores.*

Visit Silhouette Books at www.eHarlequin.com SDTFP0207